With best
wishes,

THE HOUR
GLASS

Hilary

THE HOUR GLASS

HILARY SPIERS

Published by
Pewter Rose Press
17 Mellors Rd,
West Bridgford
Nottingham, NG2 6EY
United Kingdom
www.pewter-rose-press.com

First published in Great Britain 2009

ISBN 978-0-9560053-4-2

British Library Cataloguing in Publication Data
A catalogue record for this book is available from the British Library

Cover design by www.thedesigndepot.co.uk

Printed and bound by TJ International Ltd, Padstow, Cornwall

Pewter Rose Press
www.pewter-rose-press.com

CONTENTS

Acknowledgements

Many friends and loved ones have encouraged me in my writing career, urging me on in those moments all writers experience when the self-doubts become almost overwhelming.

Foremost amongst those who have supported and encouraged me, and continue to do so, with both my fiction and playwriting are Ann and Emma Stutz, John Barrett and – of course – my husband and sons. To all those who have had faith in me, but to them in particular, my heartfelt thanks.

Several of the stories in this collection have been published previously:

- *The Hour Glass*: Winner, The Times Short Love Story Competition 2008
- *Here's Looking at You*: Winner, Sandi Toksvig's Writing Challenge 2007, Wimbledon Book Festival
- *Love-Lies-Bleeding*: Shortlisted, Bridport Prize 2008
- *Lifesaving*: Shortlisted, Writers of the Year Short Story Competition 2008
- *The Price*: Runner up, Woman & Home Short Story Competition 2006
- *Restless Pillows*: broadcast on BBC Somerset 2009
- *Seventy Times Seven*: first published in The Sorting Floor: A Lincolnshire anthology
- *Break Break Break:* First published as The Best Tunes in The Sorting Floor #2

FOREWORD

The short story is often regarded as the poor relation in terms of creative writing; this puzzles me. For the writer, the short story is a far from easy option: encapsulating a story or theme in a few thousand words – even a few hundred – demands considerable discipline and a heart hard enough to follow William Faulkner's advice to 'kill all your darlings'. For the reader, short stories offer infinite variety and a quick 'fiction fix' when time is at a premium.

If one theme unites the stories in this collection, it is relationships: between children and parents, between lovers, between pupils and teachers, between friends. A sideways glance at the everyday, the stories uncover the passions that reside in all of us, the secrets that sustain and uplift us. From children caught in the crossfire of their parents' marital wars, to the mysterious stranger found dead by the fireside, from wartime England to the heat of a summer beach, this anthology offers an eclectic mix of the comic and the tragic in life, revealing the personal in the universal.

The stories differ widely in length – some can be read in a few minutes, other demand more time. A frequent traveller, I notice that few of my fellow passengers are without some form of reading material – newspapers, novels, and, yes, even anthologies of short stories. Whether you are travelling, relaxing or simply snatching a few moments in a busy life, I hope you find something in this book that strikes a chord or raises a smile.

The Hour Glass

His hand feels warm; tiny grains of sand grind between their palms. "Look," he says, gesturing along the beach, "sand dunes. They've been here for ever." For ever, she thinks, marvelling. "They change shape and re-form every day with the sea," he says, "but they'll never disappear. They keep us safe." He squeezes her hand tight. "Come on, pumpkin, time we got back. Mummy'll be getting anxious."

She's anxious too. The looks across the sunflower-patterned cloth on the veranda table, the too-tight hugs, the silences. She fills the air with chatter, nonsense, questions, pushes books under their noses, climbs on to laps that feel cold despite the sun. Her chubby fingers trace unfamiliar lines beside mouths and eyes. Sometimes, distracted, they flick her hand away; sometimes they seize it and press it to their lips. When they do that, she snatches her hand back.

Later, in the strange bedroom, she hears their voices through the thin walls, spikes of anger breaking through the whispers. Someone is crying, muffled noises smothered by a pillow or a shoulder. Slipping from her bed, she creeps into the corridor and stands outside their door: the noises cease. Minutes pass. She pads back to her room.

The next morning, their faces are gaunt, their smiles painted on. "One last walk along the dunes," he says. Her mother turns away, fumbling for a tissue.

He strides ahead of her, oblivious to her little legs pumping to keep up. "Wait for me!" she cries, but he's too far ahead. Wind whips the words away. He stops on the shoreline, eyes fixed on the horizon. She tugs at his flapping shirt.

"Lie down, Daddy," she cries and desperately shovels sand over him. To keep him safe. To keep him there. Panicking as the grains slip through her little fingers.

HERE'S LOOKING AT YOU

But for the spot of – what? blood? rust? – on the collar, the shirt looks fine, almost new. Bit cheeky, flashy even, with those orange and pink stripes, not a combination he would have chosen, but Vin had picked it. The shoes, a curious blue – he thinks of sapphires – fit him as if custom made. Perhaps they had been – just not for him. The suit is a little baggy, but anyone could tell it was a nice bit of schmutter, as his Gran used to say. He adjusts the spotted tie, smiling at himself in the mirror. His teeth look yellow in the artificial light.

"Nah," says Vin from the doorway, startling him. The old man spins round, still nimble on his dancer's feet.

"No?"

"Not the titfer," says Vin, taking a long drag on his cigarette. Behind him hangs a large *No Smoking* sign.

"Oh." A reluctant hand creeps to his head. Until then, Terence had been confident of his hat selection, felt smart in it, a proper gent. And it looks unworn, in its own box, not like the other cast-offs, soiled with another's sweat and worse. He hesitates, feels the soft felt under his fingers. *The Bogart*, it's called. *The Bogart*, in gold letters on the smooth satin lining. "I like it. Please, son."

"Whatever." Vin isn't interested. He's edgy, distracted. "Just saying, no-one wears them no more. Not these days."

The shop assistant's heels clack along the corridor to the storeroom. "All right in there?" calls a nervous voice.

"Yeah, why?" says Vin aggressively. Terence winces.

There is a short silence. Then, "You're not smoking, are you? Only we're non-smoking now." She adds, in a rush, "Look, we don't normally let people try things on. I'm doing you a favour."

Vin crushes his cigarette out on the lino. "Be out in a minute. It's me dad. Takes him a while."

Terence stands in his socks and pants, conscious of his stale institutional smell, shrunken, vulnerable, in front of this big, angry stranger.

Vin strides ahead down the High Street, the bulging carrier bag swinging at his side. Clutching his hatbox and the cheap holdall they'd handed him that morning, Terence hurries along behind, heart thumping. Too many people, too much sky. The street is noisy with traffic and pedestrians yelling into mobile phones. He catches up with his son at the lights. Vin bounces impatiently from foot to foot, like a boxer limbering up.

"Give you a key," he says, eyes on the speeding traffic. "Bed's made up. Spare room."

"You're not coming with me?" Panic closes Terence's throat. No, he can't, can't go to a strange flat, put the key in the lock, push open the door, step through to the unknown ... It's too soon. "Vin, please ..."

"Business. Anyway, gotta stand on your own two feet." Vin's phone rings. He looks briefly at the screen, stabs a button and says, "Ten minutes." Sliding the mobile back in his pocket, he pulls out a key ring. It's a fish, enamelled, its scales articulated, so that it flexes with the weight of the key. Terence stares at it, then puts his hand out. The key drops into his creased palm, and Vin says, "10b Miles Buildings, yeah? Here," thrusting the carrier at his father.

Then he's off, across the road, dodging the hooting cars, disappearing into a narrow alley before Terence can say anything. He stands bewildered on the edge of the pavement, laden. A woman tuts as she manoeuvres round him, banging his leg with her heavy bags. He shelters in a doorway, fingering the key ring in his pocket, thumb running over the scales.

"There you go, granddad," says a young lad, laughing, thrusting a flyer into his hands as he runs past. Terence goes to drop it, but the word 'Tea' catches his eye. He's thirsty, a cup of tea would set him up, steady him. Perhaps then he'll feel better about the flat. Braver. He studies the crudely drawn map, notices the venue is only a few yards away. Picking up bags and hatbox, he launches himself with sudden courage into the human tide and is swept along to the entrance of what looks like an old cinema. A stained red carpet leads to grand marble steps, now chipped and veined with dirt. Dusty Art Deco lamps line the staircase, up which two overweight women are struggling, their swollen ankles leaking over the sides of incongruously dainty shoes. One of them turns to look down at Terence. "Don't be shy, love," she says with a throaty laugh, "We always need men." She nudges her friend and the pair of them cackle, holding on to the thick brass handrail, before hauling themselves to the top.

Terence spots the Gents sign, pushing through a battered door to the urinals. There is only one cubicle, which he enters, relishing the luxury of a lock on the door. He sits for a moment on the closed seat, calming his breathing, hugging the bags on his lap. Then he unzips his jacket.

His new clothes feel good. He feels good. Transformed. At the threshold of the ballroom, he watches the couples spin by, ageing bodies rejuvenated by skill and practised footwork. Tea and cake perfume the air. Pushing his belongings under a table, he spots the woman who spoke to him on the stairs, sitting alone, a cup in front of her. Her friend is whirling around the floor in the arms of a cadaverous old man, concentrating fiercely. The familiar music enfolds him, tugging at distant memories.

"My," says the woman with delight, as he walks over to her, muscles uncoiling, the first stirrings of confidence flowering in his heart, "who's a smartypants? I like a man in a hat. You look like a film star. Like –"

"Yes," smiles Terence, renewed, liberated. He doffs his fedora with old-fashioned gallantry. "May I have the pleasure?"

Break Break Break

Tonight is high tide. And Mary is waiting for the fall. Waiting for her house to slip like a stricken liner under the waves as the cliff on which it stands finally surrenders and crumbles in defeat. Or the land splits in a huge roar, her tiny cottage disappearing into the sea's maw, timbers screaming as they crack and tear.

She drifts from room to room, listening to the angry suck and pull of the waves far below. For forty years, this has been her home, thirty-six of them with William whose bones lie in the salty marshland graveyard a mile inland. This house too was inland once, with a long springy lawn sweeping down to the cliff path, bounded by a wire fence, to keep out the sheep and the ramblers, and beyond that, the wide capricious sea. The path, lawn, sheep and ramblers are long gone. Only the sea remains. The enemy.

"That's what comes of buying a view," jokes Mary to her nearest neighbour, Margery, snug and smug in her little bungalow beside the graveyard. Margery thinks Mary is a fool, a stubborn old fool. Mary thinks Margery is a bore. Mary sees in Margery all the qualities of old age she despises in herself. She suspects Margery does the same.

"They'll come and take you away," warns Margery. "If you don't disappear over the edge first." They are huddled over tea in Mary's precarious sitting room, Margery ensconced in the chair furthest away from the bay window.

Mary shrugs. "Let them try. I'm sound in mind and limb," she says, ignoring the nag of her arthritic knees.

"You're barking," says Margery tartly, sinking her dentures into Mary's Victoria sponge. "Anyway, just think of the mayhem. The trouble you'll cause. Do they know how bad it is?" *They* being the authorities: the officious little men (they are always men, always little, always slightly sweaty) who tut and exclaim, edging towards the drop as if afraid the ground will give way at any minute. As indeed it may.

"Oh, yes," lies Mary, ignoring the stash of letters behind the clock, all unopened, highlighted importantly in red as *EXTREMELY URGENT.*

Margery gets up to leave. "Lovely cake, dear," she says, backing towards the door and eyeing the treacherous sea nervously over Mary's shoulder. "You've seen the weather forecast?" Mary nods and follows her out to her car. As Margery bumps up the rutted track, Mary cautiously edges towards the cliff top. Another chunk of land has disappeared overnight, just under the bay window. On the beach far below, fresh, raw clay is scattered across the rocks, like the droppings of some huge bird. The sky is darkening, long skeins of grey cloud scudding along the horizon. Hungry waves lick the bottom of the cliffs. Shivering, she goes indoors.

"Mary! Darling!" the young girl says, leaping to her feet and popping the last piece of cake into her mouth. "Gorgeous cake!" And she rushes over and flings her arms around the startled old woman. Mary smells shampoo, expensive scent and is enveloped in cashmere. She feels the strong young arms around her: it's a very comforting feeling. Then reality re-asserts itself and she pulls away.

"Do I know you?" The schoolteacher in her, long dormant, resurfaces. The girl, however, is not to be cowed. She smiles charmingly.

"Not yet, darling. But you will. So lovely to meet you! Finally."

Mary is searching her memory bank. For a fleeting moment, the spectre of amnesia – worse, dementia – raises its ugly and terrifying head.

"Mary darling, do stop worrying," says the girl as if reading her thoughts. "There's nothing to fear, I promise you. Any chance of a cup of tea?"

Mary finds herself in the kitchen, filling the kettle. The girl in her soft pink sweater and tight leather trousers presses her long fuchsia-tipped fingers into the last crumbs on the cake plate and transfers them to her mouth. "This is so scrummy, Mary."

"Good," says Mary, gruffly, waiting for an explanation. Or even an introduction.

The girl licks her lips and rinses her hands under the tap, thoroughly at ease. "Right. Down to business. We'll have the tea in here, shall we? I'm not too good with heights." They sit. Mary pours two cups, as the girl repairs her makeup, expertly applying a lipstick that matches her nails.

"OK. Best be quick. There'll be a storm tonight. It's high tide. And that, I'm afraid, will be that."

"Oh," says Mary, enlightenment dawning and with it, disappointment. "You're from the bloody council."

"Council? Good God, no. Honestly!" The girl laughs, a delightful full-throated roar of incredulity. Mary finds herself almost laughing with her. "No, my darling. I'm here to make you an offer."

For one ridiculous, heart-stopping moment, Mary thinks this enchanting creature wants to buy Seaview.

"No, no, darling. Don't be daft," says the girl. "Who the hell would want to buy this place? It's falling into the sea. Tonight. Kaput. Curtains."

A great roll of thunder rattles the windowpanes. The girl stifles a scream.

"I wish they wouldn't do that!"

"Tonight?" says Mary.

"Yes! Now listen, time's running out." She whimpers as another thunderclap cracks above them, looks up and shouts, "Just stop it, you bastards." Catching sight of Mary's frown, the girl says dismissively with a flap of her hand, "History. We go back a long way," then hurries on. "OK. Here's the deal. You want to stay here? Yes?" Mary stares at her. "You want to go hurtling into the abyss as the cliff collapses?" Mary who has long resigned herself to that fate suddenly finds that she very much does not want that. She shakes her head. "Good. So the best scenario is, you remain here, so does the cliff and the sea and all three of you live happily ever after. Right?"

The kitchen is illuminated by a great bolt of lightning that flashes across the suddenly grey and boiling sea. "Oh my God!" shouts the girl, throwing her hands up in terror. "Look. Stop mucking about, will you, Mary? I'm running out of time and patience. That's the deal. Are you prepared to accept my terms?"

Mary finds her voice. It is a small, feeble thing. "In exchange for what?"

The girl looks taken aback, then cross. "Didn't I say?" Crash! goes the thunder overhead. "You see! They're trying to put me off with this storm malarkey." Leaning forward, looking into Mary's eyes, "Your soul, of course."

The sea falls silent. The thunder and lightning cease. The world stops.

"My ... soul?"

"Yes."

"But that means ..."

"Yes."

"But you're not ..."

"No."

"So you really are ...?"

"Yes," says the Devil.

"Dear God," says Mary when speech returns.

"Well, not exactly, but ... that's the gist of it," says the girl.

"What happened to ..." Mary manages a feeble gesture.

"The tail? The horns?" The girl gives a world-weary sigh. "Too mediaeval, apparently. According to the focus groups. No-one took them seriously any more."

"And aren't you supposed to be male?"

"In a patriarchal society, I guess so. But these days ... female prime ministers, presidents even ... I've been made over, as it were."

"But you're so ..."

"What?"

"Attractive."

"I know. I'm rather gorgeous, aren't I?" Just then, an unwelcome *pat-pat-pat* starts above their heads, increasing in seconds to a steady, heavy beat. "Typical! Now it's raining. Not good. Darling, I don't mean to alarm you, but I reckon we've got about twenty minutes. Thirty, tops."

"Twenty minutes for what?"

"For you to decide. Will you sell me your soul or won't you?"

"Why me? What good's my soul to you?"

"Quotas, darling. That's what it's all about these days. Have to get the numbers and frankly, the competition's enormous. There are so few decent souls left. I mean, some people positively throw themselves my way, but I don't want any old rubbish. See, if they're godless to start with, where's the victory in that? A soul's only worth having if you have to wrestle for it."

"Wrestle?" exclaims Mary, alarmed, thinking of her dodgy knees.

Again the laugh. "Oh you are so sweet, darling! Anyway, I could fix those knees of yours, if you want." Mary almost drops her cup. "No, no, no. Long dark nights of the soul, that sort of thing. That's what I meant. Only we're a bit pressed for time." The rain is getting heavier.

"So," says Mary, gulping her tea gratefully, "what exactly are you offering?"

The Devil smiles triumphantly, sensing a shift in the atmosphere. "All in good time. Just a few questions first. How would you describe your life?"

Mary thinks hard. "Boring?"

"No! In terms of how well you've behaved."

"Oh. Er ... quite well-behaved, I suppose." Then, anxiously, wanting to get things right: "You do know I don't go to church?"

"Of course. Go on."

"Oh ... well, OK, then I'd say I was ... average."

The Devil rolls her eyes and sighs theatrically. "Hopeless. Bloody hopeless."

"I'm sorry." Mary is hurt.

"No, listen, have you ever ... I don't know ... killed anyone, for example?"

"No!"

"Committed adultery?"

"No."

"Stolen anything?"

"No." A thought. "Well ..."

"Yes?" The Devil sits forward, alert as a bird of prey. "You *have* stolen something?"

Shamefacedly: "Well, when I was teaching, I used to bring home pens sometimes."

"Expensive pens?"

"No. Just the cheap ones from the stationery cupboard. Biros. You know, you just slip them in your handbag without thinking ..."

"Oh, we don't count those. Blimey, nobody would qualify if we did."

The girl puts a big tick in a box.

"I think," she says smugly, "that you're a jolly good catch, Mary. Pretty blameless life, no skeletons to speak of, just the job. All you have to do now is sign."

She holds out the pen. The rain drums down on the roof ever harder and the old cottage groans under the onslaught. Horribly loud and close, the seas boil and claw at the cliff.

"Look, don't want to rush you, but by my reckoning, the cliff's going to go in about ten minutes –"

"How do you know?"

The girl gives her a withering look. "Please."

"Sorry. So, I have to decide, do I? Right now? And the deal?"

"The cliff stays where it is. You stay on the cliff. No-one bothers you again."

"For how long? Forever?"

"Mary! I'm not a bloody miracle worker."

"I'm seventy-six now ..."

"OK. I'll give you ten years."

"Twelve. And my knees."

The Devil laughs. "You drive a hard bargain."

"And what do you get? What do you do with my soul?"

"I ..." A frown clouds the Devil's lovely face and suddenly she looks very young. "Well, I ..." She flaps an elegant hand, " ... own your soul. To do with it what I will."

"Such as ...?"

"Such as ... things."

"What sort of things?"

The Devil is rattled. "Look, I haven't got time for this shilly-shallying. The whole thing's about to go." And indeed the cottage is swaying now like a ship tossed on an angry sea, the wind prowling round its defences, looking for entry through cracks and crannies.

Mary shouts over the storm, "You can't expect me to agree without knowing the facts. I could be signing my life away!"

"You are!" The Devil shouts back. "Look, the truth is, we haven't really worked out all the details yet. I'm still waiting for the final report. Just sign, will you!" A roof tile smashes on the path; upstairs one of the casement windows is torn from its frame. Waves surge up the cliff, slapping and punching the fragile walls. Wind races through the house, billowing curtains, bowling down the hallway, as the cottage rocks and pitches. The Devil's face is white with fear and Mary's heart goes out to her. Oh, what the hell, she thinks, and reaches for the pen.

MISSING

I came face to face with myself today. One tiny image in a sea of others: the lost, the disappeared, the doomed. But it was me, beyond any doubt. The hair wasn't right – I haven't worn it long for years – but the eyes and mouth were unmistakable. My head swam, the breath knocked out of me. What was I doing in such company? Dead faces, all of them, scrubbed of emotion, like people caught unawares before they assume their daily masks. Manufactured faces, computer-aged, as blank and smooth as the paper on which they were printed. I shut the magazine abruptly, heart hammering, panic closing my throat. My mother looked up from her knitting, half an eye on the television.

"Finished with that? Let's have a gander." She held out her hand.

"No," I lied. "I'm still reading it. Tea?"

In the kitchen, I tore the page out and shoved those accelerated, imagined lives into the stove, then buried the rest of the magazine deep in the recycling pile. When I went back in with the mugs, she was wrestling with the intricacies of her pattern, swearing softly to herself.

When it comes back, as it does, as it always will, it still shocks me, after all these years. I feel myself unravelling, the ground crumbling beneath my feet. That other life, that other me, lodged like an incubus deep inside, leaves me untroubled for months sometimes and then – bam! – out it bursts, blistering my thoughts, rupturing the wound that never heals. The only certainty is its unpredictability. A panicking child crying in a supermarket, a news report, stricken parents white-faced under the camera lights, or a magazine article raking over unsolved mysteries, like today: they jolt me back to memories I cannot escape. As a teenager, I used to drink too much to forget them, subdue them. When the alcohol failed, I moved on to drugs, serious drugs: I've never been one to do things by half. Not now though, not with the baby on its way. My baby.

My distended belly rises out of the water like an island, fringed with a sudsy tide. I slide down into the bath and sink into that echoing, secret world that offers both solace and a promise of oblivion. Tendrils of seaweed hair float about my face, tracing a dance over eyes tight shut. I hum a lullaby to her, *Hold me close, don't let me go,* cradling her in the warm ocean, until I can hold my breath no longer. When I break back up to the surface, the air is cold on my skin. I gasp.

"Sweetheart!" calls my mother the other side of the door, trying unsuccessfully to disguise her anxiety. How long has she stood outside, listening, worrying? "You all right in there?"

"Fine," I say and lie back, the image of that death mask hovering on the edge of my thoughts. In the tired, steamy bathroom, black mould frames the windows, the basin tap still drips, and the toothpaste sags over the side of the mug just as it did fifteen years before ...

"We're all watching you, Suzanna!" trill the aunts, Edie in her tight leather trousers and expensive denim jacket and Cora, dreary in sensible shoes and a mac. Mum and Dad beam at their little treasure, decked out like a

Christmas tree in a spangly tutu and creamy ballet pumps, bought specially for the occasion, tiny flat chest pumping with the excitement of it all. Miss de Lamparde, the dance teacher, floats over, a vision in chiffon despite the stiff breeze, and rests her hands like a blessing on Suzanna's perfect coiffeur, tight as a skin on the fragile skull, pink scalp showing through her blonde hair. She drops a light kiss on my sister's head but we both know that while Suzanna may behave and be treated as the star of the show, she will never ever be as good as Lyndsey Barrett, shy, self-effacing, who stands to one side with her careworn mother, waiting for the pageant to begin. I've watched Lyndsey dancing when she thinks no-one is looking, when I've been dragged along to collect Suzanna after her class. Lyndsey dances as though the air is her element, her hands and arms caressing it, her feet and body in perfect harmony as the story unfolds. There's a look of rapture on her face almost too painful to bear; I see Miss de Lamparde catch it as Lyndsey practises in the corner. But today, faced with both ambitious parents and the two doting aunts, the teacher lavishes all her attention on my sister. No one takes the slightest notice of me.

I'm not complaining: that's just the way it is. Some people are blessed, that's all, knowing nothing but warmth and affection all their lives. They are at ease with the world, know no sharp corners will bruise them. The air is not cold upon their tender flesh and their lives are bounded by security and love. How is that? Where does it spring from, that confidence, that unshakeable belief in one's own worth? Suzanna has it. She's always had it. She expects, and she receives, adoration. Who would not love her, golden picture-book child, the stuff of dreams? But not me, they don't love me. I knew from the start – sensed it like a sudden draught on a summer's day – knew that I lacked the gift that makes mouths smile involuntarily, that warms a stranger's heart. No-one cooed over me in my pram, hands never reached down to muss my hair or take mine in a protective grasp. Plants wither from inattention. Perhaps I had just been sited in the wrong part of the garden, starved of the sun. I'm biddable, do largely as I am told: I learned early to push only so far, not to expect too much. I learned to watch, forever on the edge of other people's lives.

The crowd is growing by the minute, visitors and curious passers-by adding to the already heaving mass, shifting and swaying like waves behind the bigwigs' seating in search of the best view. In the front row, the town dignitaries pull their collars closer about their ears, as the biting wind bucks and swirls, insinuating its icy fingers wherever it can find entry. The Mayor smiles resolutely as his wife shivers beside him in her flimsy coat, determined to show himself above a bit of indifferent weather, waiting to enjoy the triumph of the inaugural Town Festival, his masterstroke. Miss de Lamparde's girls have been given the honour of opening proceedings with a presentation encapsulating the town's fairly insignificant history in a series of balletic tableaux. Suzanna has been practising her steps tirelessly night after night in the living room, twirling round and round in front of the television while the rest of us try to watch the screen. Or I try to watch the screen, a book, as ever, open on my lap. Of course, Mum and Dad applaud and exclaim as if her performance were taking place at Covent Garden, not in our soulless, colour co-ordinated house, among the carefully chosen furniture and accessories, all designed to display the considerable fruits of Dad's business.

He looks down at me briefly. "Don't go getting lost," he says. "You don't want to miss your sister." But I do. I don't want to watch her prancing round like a little princess, fragile as silk, while I'm bundled into one of my cousins' cast-offs, a nasty red zip-fronted cardigan with bobbles on the sleeve. It smells faintly of dog. Aunt Cora, ever conscious of her inferior status but determined not to be cowed by it, pulled it out of a bag she brought over this morning. "Here, Fiona, this'll do to keep the wind out. There's a good few years' wear left in this." She pushed me into it roughly and then waited for some response. I said nothing; just stood there mutinous in the hideous thing, with the glowering expression I know Dad hates. No-one would expect Suzanna to wear something like this, not even my aunt, as besotted with her as everyone else. Aunt Cora looked over to her sister. Mum pushed her pale hair off her forehead and sighed. I knew she wouldn't stand up to Cora: she never did. Dad, all unawares, would parade their latest acquisition – the TV, the sit-on mower – under Cora's disdainful nose. "Very nice, I'm sure," she'd sniff. "For them as can afford it." And Mum would colour, as she did now, embarrassed by our good fortune. She caught my eye, both of us thinking of the new coat hanging in my bedroom. I stared back at her, my face blank, and she looked away. "Say thank you nicely, Fiona." So I did. I did say thank you, but not nicely, I said it grudgingly, because it's charity, but then I'm a charity child whose whole life revolves around being grateful.

Dad's eyes are back on Suzanna and his hand reaches out to squeeze Mum's. She simpers like a girl and they grin at each other, a pair of idiots, faces puffed up with pride. "Look at us; look at our lovely daughter!" They don't mean me, of course. Not Fiona. The cuckoo in the nest, the outsider who intruded into their lives with typically bad timing as Mum discovered after all the years of waiting, the doctors' fingers pushing and pulling her bits, the bits they said would never support life, that she was finally, miraculously, pregnant. But it was too late: the papers were signed. I was theirs, for better or for worse. I suppose they could have sent me back, but Dad wasn't one to go back on his word, so I stayed. Not an easy baby: I was thin, colicky and I gave them months of sleepless nights. Then Suzanna, flesh of their flesh arrived, with her fluty giggle and dimples and they were lost. They tried their best. They tried to love me, but Suzanna, beautiful Suzanna, stole their hearts away and there was no room left for me.

The bodies pack tighter around me and all I can see now are waists and bums in rainbow colours. I'm bored: Aunt Cora snatched the book out of my hand as we were leaving the house and threw it on the table. "For goodness sake, Fiona, put that wretched thing down! You can't read in the street." Yes, you can, *I* can, I can read anywhere. Reading opens up the world, transports and seduces me, makes me believe anything is possible. I feel bereft without a book in my hand. Lonely. I read in bed when I'm supposed to be asleep, listening out for Mum's footsteps on the stairs. She takes her shoes off at the bottom and creeps up to catch me out. "It's for your own good. You'll go blind reading in the dark," she says, which is stupid. You're only using your eyes, just as if you were looking at the television or reading the labels in the supermarket. Instead of standing here

21

getting cold and cross, I could be buried in my book now, miles, continents, centuries away from here. I wouldn't feel the cold then.

Dad tries to ease me to the front where I'll be able to see better but I wriggle and writhe until he gives up and says crossly, "For heaven's sake, stand still, Fiona. And where on earth did that come from? Where's your new coat?" I shrug. "Aunt Cora gave me this. Mum said I had to wear it." He gives a snort of disgust. "Well, hold on to me and don't go wandering off." So I do as I'm told, hanging on to the sleeve of his jacket for a few minutes, while more and more people jostle for a vantage point and I am buffeted by the elbows and handbags of impatient onlookers. All through the Mayor's opening speech, the family waves furiously at Suzanna, standing arrow-straight in the front row, waiting for her cue. Obedient to instructions and mindful of her responsibilities, Suzanna, unlike many of her fellow dancers, refuses to reciprocate. A neighbour slaps Dad on the back and bellows a greeting in his ear as the crowd burst into whoops and whistles, applauding the band marching smartly into the square.

As people surge forward, I gently let go of Dad's sleeve and eel my way through legs and bags dumped on the ground to the edge of the crowd. Shopkeepers are standing on the steps of their stores watching the spectacle. A woman presses up against the inside of the hairdresser's window, towel trailing from a shoulder, one side of her head prickled with rollers, while the stylist, comb in hand, waits impatiently behind her. The air is thick with the sickly smell of sugared oil from the doughnut stall. Up strikes the band and everyone turns to look at the musicians in their bright uniforms and the little dancers taking up their positions. And in that moment, as the whole world seems transfixed by the sight of these pretty creatures in their dainty costumes and the great clash of drums and blasts of trumpets fill the square, I see them.

She has her arm through his as if she needs him to support her. There is something in his face that tells me he relishes that need. And I know suddenly and with utter certainty, that this closeness, this mutual dependency, is incomplete, is waiting for the last piece of the jigsaw to fall into place, to heal them. There's a sorrow in her eyes, and his, a sorrow, almost a hunger, as they stare across the heads of the crowd at the girls holding hands in a circle, waiting to begin their dance. It's as if I can see inside their heads, the ache and longing for small arms around their necks, the comfort of a soft, warm body in their laps.

Years later, they said to me, "How did you know? You were six! How did you know you'd be safe with us?" And I laughed, triumph bubbling in my throat, and said, "I just did."

And I was right. They did keep me safe, or as safe as any parents can keep their child. They loved me unconditionally, indulged me, endured my tantrums, lavished praise and attention on me, caught me when I fell and sacrificed their own lives to make mine as perfect as it could be. And I repaid them cavalierly, cruelly, as only children confident of love can, with indifference and neglect, with insults and silence. I left, I came back, I stayed away, I stayed too long. But I loved them then and I love them still. And every time I walk through the door into that shabby terraced house, red-eyed, angry and finally, pregnant, they open their arms without a word and enfold me, welcoming me home.

When I was fourteen, I found the curled, faded clippings from the newspapers hidden at the back of their wardrobe in an old biscuit tin. I pored over the reports of my disappearance, the same sad photo, all glasses and pigtails, staring out of dozens of news reports and read with guilty pleasure the profiles of the paedophile who had surely snatched me, done unspeakable things to my defenceless body and then buried my corpse deep where no-one would ever find me. There were pictures of Mum and Dad weeping at press conferences, Mum pathetically clutching some grubby soft toy that I had never liked but which the papers had invested with some mystical significance. I was no longer Fiona, I was little Fee, the creation of the reporters for whom every abducted child is an angel, unsullied, perfect. "We'll never stop hoping," sobbed Mum in a tearful interview, describing my untouched bedroom and my grieving sister, pictured inevitably in her ballet clothes. Classmates who had never spoken to me left misspelled messages of sorrow pinned to teddy bears at the school gates and a forest of flowers bloomed there for a few days. Did Suzanna, did Mum and Dad, did the aunts, think of me still?

In the days following the pageant, I would hear Mummy and Daddy – my new, so grateful parents – whispering tearfully that I must be taken back and I would fly into their bedroom, air cold on my newly naked neck, throw myself between them in the yeasty bed and sob and sob, pleading with them to be allowed to stay here, here where I was loved, here where I was wanted. I was cunning, old beyond my years; it was I who invented a distant dying cousin begging for her soon-to-be-orphaned little daughter to be given a home, I who settled quickly, joyfully, into my new life with my new parents, making sure everyone we met knew how happy I was. When they wanted to flee, to move far away, I stopped them. Where better to hide a missing child than where she was lost? We lived in the nearby city so I changed schools, that was all – and changed personality. I transformed myself overnight from sullen wraith to boisterous, mischievous tomboy. And as the days and then the weeks passed, it became more and more impossible to imagine the journey to the police station, the confessions, the prosecution and inevitable imprisonment. For who would believe me, the victim? Believe that I had chosen my new Mummy and Daddy, as my adoptive parents had once chosen me, and that I wanted to spend my life with them, as adored and cosseted as Suzanna?

I slip silently behind the crowd as the dancing starts, the air punctuated with little oohs and ahs of pleasure and admiration. She sees me first. She nudges him and whispers something in his ear, as a look of first pleasure, then anxiety, flashes across her face. Then he turns to look at me too. I smile, a smile that I know lights up my face, a smile I have practised endlessly in front of the wardrobe mirror. They both smile back.

They are standing a little apart from the crowd, isolated on a corner. I recognise that diffidence, the lack of confidence; rejection teaches you to keep your distance. I start to cross the space between us, as if pulled by an invisible string. On an uneven paving stone, I stumble, falling hard to my knees, feeling the skin break. I hear her exclaim and they both run towards me. When they reach me, blood is already welling from the wound. I don't cry though; I just reach up and she puts her arms around me, her sweet, musky smell in my nostrils. Her skin is dry and soft, her eyes kind, framed with tiny wrinkles.

"Whoopsadaisy, sweetheart," she says. "Dear oh dear, what have you done?"

The blood blooms on my knee like a jewel; when she presses it with her handkerchief I feel it spreading, warm on my skin. I don't speak: just stare up at her with wide eyes, tears threatening.

"What's your name, poppet?"

I hesitate, but only for a second. Something clicks in my head. "Felicity," I say, out of nowhere.

She gasps and begins to tremble, the blood draining from her cheeks. She looks up at the man bending over us both. In their tangled glances, pain and shock intermingle. "Felicity!" she breathes as the ghost of my namesake, their dead daughter, looks on.

Did I know? How could I? How, out of the thousands of names, could I have known to choose that one? Felicity. Dead in twenty-four hours from meningitis just before her sixth birthday. Precocious, bookish and plain. Just like me.

She looks into my face, as if searching for something, the answer to an unspoken question. "That's a ... pretty name." Her voice cracks. Gently, reverently, she puts out a hand and cradles my face. "Felicity," she repeats, like a prayer. He puts a hand on her shoulder, a big, safe, comforting hand. She looks up at him, then back at me and slowly, slowly withdraws her fingers from my cheek. I hold her gaze, eyes locked on to hers as our tears spill and mingle on our clasped hands. The rest will be easy.

BLITZ E15

Number 17

When it falls, she is dressing her hair, magazine open on the table, tongue clamped between her teeth in concentration, mirroring the pictures in her mirror. She twists the hank of thick brown hair in one hand, enjoying its weight, then slides the pin up like a knife through butter. She likes the secret hollow of her armpit, the way the light through the window haloes the fine hairs on her arms. Her free hand drops to her waist, caresses the warm silk. She imagines other hands there, hard hands, urgent, holding her tight. She imagines –

The mirror dissolves, sliding down the wall like a sigh, as the window explodes and the house convulses, haemorrhaging brick and wood and glass. A million tiny knives *snick snick snick* slice back, legs, arms and hands neat as a surgeon. Was there a siren? She didn't hear it, can hear nothing for the present, just peer through the dusty fog to find the door and totter in unsteady heels to the edge of the abyss that was once a house. Far below, her brother, plastered like a saint, lies neat as nine pence in his bed on the kitchen table. Above him, the evening sky, edged in red. Fine day tomorrow. "Awright, sis?" he yells, his eyes black holes in the dust of his face. "What larks!" A beam lies across his legs.

She picks a delicate way down what remains of the stairs and stumbles out into the shattered street, where dust swirls and bewildered neighbours begin to emerge into the dying light. Her hand finds the wall, railings long gone, and she subsides onto the bricks. Their surface is rough through the shredded fabric; the wall feels wet and her teeth chatter. Through the haze, across the street, windows gape, glass carpets the road. A warden materialises beside her. "Christ, Jim!" he shouts, "Over 'ere. This one's bad."

Gently, gently, as her brother calls her name, the man's strong, capable hands close around her waist.

Number 23

When it falls, Betty and Joan are playing in the cave. It is dark in their tented kingdom, bounded by the four ugly Victorian legs. They scream – they're only little – but Ma is up the road for a loaf and no-one answers. Only the initial explosive thud and the buckle and fall of masonry, then the trickle of falling debris.

Betty pokes a head out. Shattered furniture blocks their escape. "Best wait for Ma," she says, eight and serious. "Wait for Ma," echoes Joan, six, lying like an effigy on the lumpy mattress.

Suddenly, their mother's voice, unhinged by fear, calls out, as she claws over the wreckage outside their tomb. "Girls! Girls!"

Betty shouts, "We're all right, Ma. But we can't get out. Oh, and one of the castors's broken." The girls can hear new voices, their mother calling the men over, desperate. "My girls are trapped in there. They say they're safe. What happened? There was no warning," she cries, bewildered.

"Bastards weren't after us. For a change. Just dropping their leftovers on their way home. Come on, missus. Just step away so we can get a bit of light – oh! Don't move! Stay right where you are, love. We've got some live wires across the hall here. Just stand still. George, I need a hand."

"Girls, girls," says their mother, her mouth to the keyhole. "They'll have you out in a jiffy. Stay calm."

"Stay calm," Betty instructs her sister.

"I am calm," says Joan, indignant, hands palm to palm on her chest. "Look at me being calm."

Twenty minutes later, a precarious channel is cleared to the table. The girls are pulled into their mother's suffocating embrace. "Ma," says Betty crossly, "you're all dusty. And your hair's gone grey." Ma laughs, Joanie laughs, they all laugh. The girls gaze round in wonder at the wreckage of their home as the firemen hurry them out. "Got somewhere to go, have you? Only there's a shelter down by the Underground." Ma sniffs. "Got relatives in the next street we have," she says. "Ta ever so, though." No time for sentiment: they set off for Aunty Peg's, the girls eager for an audience for their adventure.

Aunt Peg is standing in her doorway, broom in hand, surveying the damage, most of which she appears to have swept into the garden. Not too bad: all her windows are out, but Uncle Tom is already hammering temporary boards across them. She nods with grim satisfaction at the sight of her sister and nieces safe and unharmed, then beckons them to follow her as she gingerly makes her way to the scullery at the back of the house.

"I'll rustle us up something to eat. Betty, look and see what's left in the larder."

The floor and shelves are littered with tins and broken jars of preserves, chutneys and pickles, all covered thickly with dust. Betty blows as hard as she can to clear some of it which sends most of it straight into her face and sets her off on a prolonged bout of coughing.

"Come on, girlie," shouts Aunt Peg, "Ain't got all day. Anything left?"

"Only these," says Betty, bringing out a bowl of eggs. A dusty dozen. Unbroken.

Number 16

When it falls, she's with a client. He slipped in like a wraith, but the old boy across the way was standing by his window as usual and caught a glimpse. Well, good luck to him.

She knows what they think of her, the neighbours. It used to worry her. Now it slides off her like a slick of oil, just another cross to bear in a mountain of crosses. After what she's seen, what's a bit of gossip, the odd spiteful comment here and there? Once someone spat at her as she passed, the gob of phlegm hitting her cheek like a blow. "Bloody foreigners." Still, if that's the worst they can do …

She keeps herself to herself, hugging walls, eyes to the pavement as she flits out into the dusk every night. But not tonight. Tonight's different. She has the house to herself and he's here, now, in the privacy of her own home.

He wastes no time. The minute the door closes, he pulls her towards him. She'd like to say, "Stop, let's talk first. Get to know each other." But his hands are insistent. Lust girdles their hot young flesh, mouth on mouth, bone to bone. He knows what she is, but she can make herself believe that there is only the now, only the present, that his incoherent gasps are something more than animal. Fingers splay, clench, stroke and scratch, raking the glistening skin like ploughs biting the dark earth. She wants him to say something tender, but he is desperate now as though time is running out.

"Hold me," she wants to say. Memories crowd in, another time and world when she belonged, was not the outsider, when family protected her and kept her safe. There was sunlight then, before the clouds gathered, before that enchanted life was fractured forever by the man with the silly moustache. She strokes his springy hair, a million happy miles away.

"Oh, baby," he groans, her hand on his fragile skull like a blessing, defenceless in the bitter sunless air. Secret, sly, wreathed in darkness, she smiles. "Oh honey!" he moans.

"Esther," she says. But softly.

The screams of man and bomb collide in a single note of death.

Number 18

When it falls, she is staring at the sky, standing in the garden where bruised apples gape with wasp-burrows, sweet with rot. The crumbled walls bleed into earth that is soured by resentful London light.

She remembers the sensation of hunger, but cannot summon its reality. Thin blades of bone protrude beneath the homemade dress, as she fingers a discarded doll, blind eyes bright with tears. She found the doll this morning, stuffed behind the dressing table. Connie, no doubt, trying to keep her treasures safe from Mary's marauding hands. Hidden and then forgotten. The bedroom still holds a drift of sweat and sweetness that breaks and comforts their mother's heart every time she enters.

Her absent daughters shout and scream in her mind, their soft limbs entwined round hips that ache with emptiness. She is still not convinced she did the right thing, sending them away. To have them here, together, to hold them, comfort them, isn't that better than this terrible fear that never leaves her, the nightmare and the guilt?

Oh, they write cheerfully enough, but who's to say that's not the people they're with, making them say these things? A pile of childish letters, bubbling with delight at hedges, livestock and horizons, the milking of a cow, pulling your own dinner out of the ground! *Ma, it's fantastic!* Will it change them, this new life? Will they come back, plump with cream and beef, sturdy strangers? "Don't you worry, Mrs P, they'll be right as rain, you'll see." How could they be so sure? She's already lost a husband, doesn't want to lose all she has left, but they nag and press her, smile their relentless smiles and she surrenders.

It don't half rain a lot here, Ma, they write in blotted strokes. *Got proper soaked on Sunday.* The proof a clumsy picture of Mary, pigtails and ribbons coloured in with care, and drops of rain all around her. She hugs it to her bosom and Mary is soaked once more.

The birds fall silent, their evening chorus stilled. Red as blood, the sun descends behind the houses, as another sound dread and familiar fills the air. The sky, heavy with hate, sheds its deadly silver drops.

In Devon, rain falls soft as silk upon her wide-eyed girls.

Number 2

When it falls, Sidney Smith – Private Smith, 65, ex First Battalion, The London Regiment – is watching a rat. Alone in his shabby terraced house, isolated by bitterness and pride, knife-sharp seams flat against knife-sharp knees, beaky nose aloft, he watches a rat watching him from its skirting-board trench. He knows the bastard and its family, from mean black eyes to sinister tail. He knows it like a lover: the thrust of its nose, brush of its whiskers, nip of its teeth and its greed for flesh.

They're old friends, him and the rat. Old foes. Not just this rat, of course, but any rat. He's seen enough of them. "To last me a lifetime," he used to say when he came back from the last war.

When you've seen them at work on the battlefield, among the corpses, you've got their measure. They're indefatigable, rats. Nothing keeps them out. God knows he's tried. And now he has a sort of grudging respect for them. It's like they're reluctant comrades. *Whither thou goest*, he thinks to himself, out of nowhere. They both know death, both know this Hitler geezer is all piss and wind.

Night falls on the broken street, cloaking the dead and the living. There is a kind of beauty and grandeur in the jagged remains, still reaching defiantly into the sky. Tomorrow, another lovely day accordingly to the sunset. They'll make the most of it, the survivors, so as not to waste a minute, so as to be ready for the next deadly cargo when it falls.

LIFESAVING

"All right?" says the man, his breath overpowering but oddly sweet, mouth a red, wet cavern. She shrinks away, startled by his bristly face in hers. The rough seat prickles the backs of her legs and she has to stop herself from wriggling. His breath slithers around her like a scummy tide; she tries not to breathe in. Her tiny pink toes do an involuntary dance of terror on the suede linings of her new wedges. But she is a polite little girl, in her pretty tiered skirt and denim jacket. She stares back at him, nodding, eyes unreadable in a set white face.

"Be there soon," he says, his tongue slipping out for a lazy wipe of his lips. He squints as the sun flicks past the pylons in blinding jabs of light. His eyes close for a moment, then he snaps them back open. "You like cake?"

She starts, shakes her head, pressing back even further into her seat, eyes sliding across the aisle to a fat lady lost in a baguette and a lurid magazine. Crumbs and tomato pips fall in a steady stream on to her broad bosom straining against the confinement of her green tee shirt. *Hot stuff* says the legend picked out in silver sequins. The little girl likes the sequins, but knows her mother would not. She wishes her mother were with her now.

The man sits back in his seat and bares his teeth in a yawn. His front tooth sparkles. She blinks. Is that a diamond? He taps the tooth with his index nail. "Fancy not liking cake. All kids like cake." He sounds puzzled. Disappointed. The fat woman shovels the last piece of bread into her mouth with the heel of her hand and glances over. She catches him eyeing her chest and heaves herself together in high dudgeon, brushing down her affronted breasts. The man snorts and looks back at the little girl, cocking his head in the woman's direction as if to say, "What's she like, eh?" Something roguish in his eye makes the little girl relax, she almost smiles.

"That's better. Now we're getting somewhere." The woman looks over again. "My princess," he says and winks. The woman sniffs and turns her head away.

At their station, he gets up without a word and she follows, heaving her case off the rack by the door. As the train judders to a halt, he puts his meaty hand on her shoulder; she notices his nails are rimmed with grime. Again, that waft of something sweet, decaying, as he grunts heavily, climbing the steps to the bridge across the line. She struggles with her heavy case; he doesn't seem to notice. It bangs painfully on her leg in time with her feet. Catching the last uneven step, he loses his footing, and as he almost falls, instinctively she reaches out to catch him. Leaning on her hard as he regains his balance, his fingers bite into her thin upper arm. "Whoopsadaisy!" he laughs nervously, shepherding her through the gateway in the stone wall, tossing their tickets in the general direction of the waste bin. They flutter to the ground and she goes back to pick them up and drop them in, while he waits and then starts walking. She trots along at his side, silent.

"Getting tired?" he says after a few minutes, panting himself. "Not far now." His shoelace has come undone but he hasn't noticed. She says nothing. They round a corner and come to a rundown row of terraced cottages, the one at the end more dilapidated than the rest, a blanket tacked

35

up haphazardly in the window, the front door splintered and rotten. He puts a key in the lock and then shoves hard with his shoulder so the door bursts open, releasing a foetid mixture of stale air and the smell of damp. He steers her inside and slams the door behind them. In the darkness of the hallway all she can hear is his laboured breath and the rattle of phlegm in his chest. A tiny whimper escapes her before she can stop it.

"Whoa, whoa, little girl," he whispers hoarsely, reaching out to stroke her head. She flinches and moves away, tripping over a pile of old newspapers, pushing open the door at the end of the hall. Sunlight pours out, refracted through the dust swirling in the disturbed air. She takes in a squalid kitchen, surfaces littered with dirty plates and pans, opened tins, pizza boxes, foil containers. Flies swim lazily in the soupy air. They crawl over a dented box balanced on the crowded table, containing a party cake, Smarties bleeding into the yellowing icing. She looks up at him, then away.

"Yeah, yeah, needs a bit of a tidy. We'll sort it. The pair of us." Clumsily, he starts to shovel the rubbish into a bulging black bin bag. One of the foil containers slices through the thin plastic and the contents explode across the greasy floor, scattering stinking garbage at their feet. He swears angrily, falling back into the hallway. She hears him stagger into the front room and the heavy thud as he collapses into a chair.

A few grains of rice, grey and oily, sit on her new shoes like tiny grubs. She bends down to flick them off and, through the open door of the cupboard below the sink, catches sight of some ancient shrivelled rubber gloves. She pulls them out and slides their cold puckered skins over her small hands. She thinks of her mother's gloves, neat, clean, sweet-smelling, hanging over the side of the sink. She swallows hard.

When he surfaces from his troubled dreams, brain clouded, his tongue feels thick and coated. He looks around at the heaps of old books, the broken curtain rail propped up in the corner, the surfaces thick with dust. It's all too much. The thought of doing something, anything, is too huge to contemplate. Better to close down, take another slug. His hand gropes across the stained carpet but the bottle he finds is empty. He groans, sitting forward on the chair, his throbbing head in his hands, trying to clear the jumble in his mind. Fragments of memory slip and slide about, like oil on water. The officious woman at the hospital, taking his papers so gingerly, her mouth pursed with distaste. The inspector on the train, checking and re-checking their tickets. The little girl shrinking into her seat. The little girl ...

Unfamiliar noises, quiet but urgent, come from the kitchen. Levering himself upright, he moves unsteadily down the hall, silently pushes the door open and stands on the threshold. The air smells different. It is fresh with the sharp tang of cleaner and bleach. She is standing barefoot on a spotless draining board carefully wiping the grime from the windows. Her tiny shoes sit neatly in the corner on the pristine floor. There is no sign of the cake. Three black bags wait by the kitchen door. He watches her for a few moments, the rhythm of her arms echoing a distant past, another window.

"Hungry?" he croaks. She jumps at the sound of his voice, pauses in mid-wipe, but does not turn. Just nods, then carries on with the task. He wishes she would turn, acknowledge him. "I'll nip out. Get some grub. You be OK?" She carefully eases her feet round to face him, silhouetted in the afternoon light and looks at him gravely. She seems so small, her feet delicate and fragile, her eyes dark smudges in her pallid face. He wants the face to smile, wants those thin arms round his neck, wants to hold her tight; the violence of his longings frightens him. All at once he is aware of his sour smell, the stubble on his chin. He turns and stumbles up the stairs to the bathroom. Running icy water into the filthy basin, he washes himself as best he can, relishing the cold air on his wet skin, scrubbing feverishly with the nailbrush, his shaking hands dragging a razor hurriedly over his skin. He dabs at the nicks with scraps of toilet paper, leaving some of them stuck to his face. The toothpaste on his teeth tastes good.

When he gets back from the takeaway, the blanket is gone from the front window. The glass gleams. A stepladder stands in the hall. In the kitchen, two places have been laid, and tumblers stand beside a jug he did not know he owns. He takes the containers out of the carrier bag and puts them carefully on the mats, then pulls out the quarter bottle of whisky. Just as he goes to unscrew the top, he sees her face. She is looking at him unblinkingly; he recognises that look. He pushes the bottle away.

She eats very little, fastidiously, like a cat, he thinks. The rake of their forks across the plates sounds unnaturally loud in the silent kitchen. Between them, the unopened whisky bottle sits on the table like a challenge. When they have both finished, she climbs down from her chair and stacks the plates, carrying them over to the sink like precious crystal. She picks up the rubber gloves.

"Leave it," he says. "We'll do them later. Together." He remembers the basin upstairs. "Anyhow, I need them. Do the bathroom." Her silence begins to unnerve him. "Come here." Still clutching the gloves, she walks over to him, stands in front of him, watchful, waiting. The whisky bottle is so close; he can taste it. He takes another sip of water.

"Listen, we'll manage, yeah?" She looks down and he does likewise, examining his hands, surprised to see them clean, pleased at the sight. "Right little worker, aren't you? Good girl. Like everything all shipshape and Bristol fashion, eh? Just like your ..." An image, vivid as a photo, flashes up in his thoughts then dissolves. But the shadow it leaves behind offers an odd comfort. "Think I'm a bit of a slob, eh? Letting things slide and that. It's just ... it's easier to ... when you live alone." He flicks a glance at the bottle. Her eyes are still fixed upon his face. He wants to fathom that look. "I know it's all a bit strange. Bound to be. I'm sorry that I've ... I mean, I've not been well, see, not since ... it's not that I didn't care. About you, I mean. I did. I do." She blinks and bites her lip. A tiny pulse throbs in her throat. "Have to tell me what to do, won't you? What you like. Food. Clothes. Stuff like that. Show me how to clean, eh?" She thrusts the gloves at him and reaches over to the sink to hand him the Cif. He barks a chesty laugh. "Right. Starter's orders. Best get on."

As he is getting to his feet, there is a knock at the front door. They both freeze: she is the first to move but as she goes towards the hall, he grabs her by the hand. He feels her stiffen. "Georgie, look, about your Mum. I'm so sorry. I'll do my best. I will." A tiny uncertain smile flickers across her face and as she turns, he thinks he can see a tear trembling in her eye. Perhaps it's the light. Then she pulls her hand away, but gently, and slips into the hall.

He hears her tugging at the door, then a stranger's voice, high, professional. "Hello, you must be Georgina. I've come to see how you're getting on. Can I come in?"

He holds his breath, suddenly afraid of being judged unworthy, unfit. Not by the woman, but by her. Then, light as air, swelling his head and chest with an emotion that threatens to both save and undo him, she calls out, clear and sweet, "Dad!"

THE PRICE

Now I am cabin'd, cribbed, confined, Sarah thought suddenly, as the familiar *Frost* theme tune started and David Jason's face peered out quizzically through the bars. The words circled round her head, her mind snagging on them like a broken tooth. The imagery startled her. No, she reasoned, trying to concentrate on the storyline which seemed disappointingly familiar, that's ridiculous: Macbeth's cry is one of thwarted ambition. My surrender is entirely willing. A future of love, companionship and security, not something to be sniffed at by a fifty-four year old long-term divorcee, a little weathered and tending toward the matronly. The unbidden phrase however unsettled her. Finally, utterly distracted, she mentioned it to George beside her on the sofa. Her favourite armchair had long since been relegated to the far corner.

He sat up, the warmth of his body as he shifted away an immediate and painful loss.

"You really feel that?"

His obvious distress dismayed her. "Not exactly. I'm not going to knock off my best mate and seize the throne. I meant it metaphorically, I suppose."

He picked up her hand with its still unfamiliar diamond ring and, gently smoothing the paint-flecked skin, said tightly, "Are you having second thoughts?"

Sarah paused before replying. The option of throwing herself into his arms seemed at once juvenile and too easy. She angled her body towards him on the couch. This really wasn't as comfortable as her old armchair. "No. Not second thoughts. But thoughts, yes. Of course I am thinking about it. It will mean a great deal of change. I'm used to calling all the shots, remember."

"I thought you liked change."

"I do like change. But change can be anything from a new car to a new life. I think this is a bit more than the latest model."

"Are we talking cars or men?"

She withdrew her hand.

"Are we having our first quarrel?"

He bent down to pick up the bottle and refilled his glass, checking first that hers was still full.

"Quarrel? Aren't we a bit old for that? Quarrels are for incontinent youngsters, not boring old farts like us."

She bridled. "Speak for yourself. All I'm saying is that this feeling, this sensation, is bothering me." She knocked back a slug of wine. He looked at her for a moment, then leant across to kiss her on the lips. She could taste the wine on both their breaths. It was good wine. It was a good kiss.

"Sarah, I want to make a life with you, make you happy. As happy as you make me. Isn't that enough?"

"It'll just have to do," she said in an attempt at levity, instantly regretted, as a look of pain flickered momentarily in his eyes.

"Sorry. Sorry. Fatal personality flaw: when in a corner, opt for facetiousness. More wine?" And getting up to go into the kitchen, she managed both to apologise inadequately and then trivialise the apology. Oh dear, she thought, rummaging noisily through the wine rack, at our age this love business is harder than I thought.

George materialised beside her and took the corkscrew from her hand. She let him. A year, a month ago even, she wouldn't have, but now ... It felt good to be cosseted. Leaning back against the work surface, she watched him deftly ease the cork from the bottle, pour a glass and hand it to her. "You not having one?"

George shook his head. "No, not if we're off first thing."

The glass, halfway to her lips, came to a halt. "Tomorrow? Are you going to run me to the station?"

"No, I thought we'd drive."

Carefully, she put the glass down.

"Darling, I'm going to take the train. I'm meeting Mandy at Waterloo."

"Yes, I know. I just thought it might be more convenient to have the car?"

"In London? Don't be daft. Anyway ..." Sarah wasn't quite sure how to frame this, but she wanted to be quite clear. "You're not coming." That sounded rather peremptory, so she added, "Are you?"

George frowned, looked almost affronted. "Darling, we've loads of things to get for the wedding. You haven't even decided on your dress yet."

Sarah thought fast. "George, I haven't seen Mandy for ages. We weren't thinking of going shopping. There's an exhibition on at the Tate we thought we'd like to see and then –"

"Great! I saw that in the paper. I thought you and I might pop down. But of course Mandy will be most welcome. I hadn't realised she was into art like us. Well, like you, I should say. I'm just a new recruit. I'm really looking forward to meeting her."

Sarah smiled inwardly, and sighed. It wasn't worth upsetting him. He was a dear, dear man, generous to a fault, loving and considerate. And if he really couldn't bear to be parted from her for a day, shouldn't she be flattered?

He put his arms around her. "I can't believe this, sometimes. How quickly it's all happened. The way everything just *fits*." Perhaps, thought Sarah, tonight was not the best time to retreat to her studio until the early hours.

If Mandy was surprised when her old friend appeared at the barrier with a tall, smiling stranger, she didn't show it. Within minutes George had a woman on either arm as they strolled to the taxi rank. He was in his element.

"What a treat. Not one but two gorgeous women for the day. Mandy, I'm relying on you to get this wretched creature into something classy for the big day. Left to her own devices, she'd be in jeans and a tee shirt. Probably spattered with paint."

Sarah was about to defend herself when she caught sight of Mandy's flushed face wreathed in a coquettish smile. Really, she thought, middle-aged women are such suckers. Her irritation increased as George slyly winked at her friend. Pulling her arm away, Sarah said rather brusquely, "Can you hang on a tick while I nip to the loo?"

"Here?" said George, as if the station toilets were only slightly more salubrious than an open sewer. "Darling, please, let's go to an hotel and you can use the facilities there. We could have coffee." Mandy brightened immediately. Sarah felt her hackles rise. "Two minutes," she said and shot off across the concourse.

When she returned, Mandy and George were getting on famously. What on earth was Mandy doing with her handbag, plaiting the strap like a love-struck schoolgirl? Piqued, Sarah strode past them towards the taxis, saying over her shoulder, "Tate first?" Hurrying after her, George said mischievously with a glance at Mandy, "Sweetheart, I'm so sorry, didn't realise you were back. Your friend is distracting me." Mandy gave a rather shrill laugh and screwed up her face into an expression Sarah had never seen before and certainly didn't wish to see again. She repeated her suggestion.

Was it her imagination, or did Mandy's face fall a fraction? Sarah leaned towards her. "I said, shall we start with the exhibition?"

Mandy looked up at George. What was she expecting, guidance? Sarah let out an exasperated breath, "What? Don't you want to go?" Mandy dragged her eyes away from George's face and looked confused. No, worse than confused, helpless. "I thought George said we were going shopping."

"Coffee first," said George determinedly and ushered them both into a cab. Sarah capitulated. Coffee would be nice, she admitted. Coffee, then the exhibition.

"What a lovely day," said George, loading the bags into the car boot at the station. "Isn't Mandy delightful? Pity about the exhibition. Still, we can pop down next week perhaps. And that dress is going to look fabulous on you. Does look fabulous on you. No, you look fabulous in it."

"Thanks," said Sarah, ungraciously. Five hours in Harrods and Harvey Nicks. Her feet throbbed as if the devil himself were prodding her with his fork. Catching sight of the dress's price tag, she had felt almost sick and had had to walk away – dragging Mandy – when George presented his credit card. And as for the underwear, the negligée, the shoes ... There was no denying they were lovely, but all that money ...

George settled into the evening traffic and leaned across to squeeze her hand. "I thought tomorrow we might start looking for somewhere to go on honeymoon. You know, get some brochures? Look on the internet? Anywhere you fancy?"

Gingerly, Sarah eased her feet in her shoes and stared out unseeingly at the Hampshire countryside flashing by. "Cornwall," she said, picturing crashing waves, seagulls wheeling above tiny harbours, wild moors, the sky. Her hands itched for her brushes.

"Cornwall?" said George, incredulous. "In May? I meant somewhere special. Anywhere. Your heart's desire."

"Cornwall is my heart's desire," said Sarah. "I love it."

George skilfully manoeuvred the car past a tractor and then pulled smoothly into a lay-by. He switched off the engine and turned to Sarah.

"Darling, listen to me. I want to give you everything. I *can* give you everything. I know you've had to be careful in the past, but, honestly, you don't need to worry any more. I can give you material things, whatever you want, but you give me so much more. Love, laughter, a sense of belonging. Mine's a poor return for all of that. I won't say you've got me to look after you now, because, God knows, you're not a woman who needs looking after. But I want you to have everything you've ever dreamed of. I just want to spoil you to death." He started up the engine and drove on home. Sarah sat very quiet, the soles of her feet on fire.

They settled on a safari. It looked beautiful in the brochures.

The wardrobe in the spare bedroom bulged with holiday clothes. Expensive holiday clothes. Sarah's scruples seemed to have taken a holiday themselves. The prudence of an impoverished artist's life, under the influence of George's generosity and encouragement, gave way with alarming ease to excess. ("Manolos, Ma! Oh my God. Can I borrow them?" said Katie.) Sarah hadn't painted anything for weeks, too busy planning the quiet family wedding that had grown somehow into a sit-down meal for three hundred with band, marquee, MC ("An MC, Ma? You'll be playing bridge next!") extravagant floral displays, co-ordinated linen and tableware and fireworks at midnight. Caterers, entertainers and florists tramped through the door day after day, weaving round groups of awe-struck, breathless friends, many of whom George had reintroduced to her life after trawling through old address books. They were astonished at the new Sarah, chic and sophisticated, as astonished as she was herself. They all loved George.

"Isn't he scrummy?" the women whispered behind their hands. "God, how lucky is Sarah?" Mandy, an early convert, felt herself especially privileged, dispensing scraps of gossip whenever Sarah was out of the room. "Lost his first wife. Cancer. Tragic. Met Sarah at the theatre. Coup de foudre. Amazing." Yes, it was, they all agreed, amazing. Some of them were unable to suppress the tiniest, meanest niggle of envy that Sarah, who had always been so, well, ordinary – talented, undoubtedly, but no fashion plate, let's face it – should be the lucky recipient of such largesse. Of such devotion, too. For Heaven's sake, the man absolutely doted on her. And didn't he fit in well? They eyed their own men with veiled resentment.

Sarah looked round her newly decorated sitting room. It pained her to admit it, but George had done a far better job than she would have. Everything was quietly expensive, discreetly tasteful. It spoke of money, subtly spent. She still wasn't sure if she liked what he'd done with her paintings, concentrating them all on one wall. She always felt her work needed room to breathe.

"I've invited the Harpers over for supper on Saturday," said George, handing her a champagne flute. "Thought it would be good to catch up with them."

Sarah had to think for a minute before she could place them. Good Lord, she hadn't seen Cynthia for years, not since they had been at art school together in London. As for her husband – Eric was it? – she wasn't sure they'd ever met.

"Right," she said uncertainly.

George smiled, misreading her hesitation. "No need for you to worry, darling – I'm cooking. The Smiths are coming too. And Mandy and Phil, of course."

Sarah frowned. "I'd no idea you knew the Smiths."

George gave her a wry look. "I told you. I rang them out of the blue the other week, to introduce myself. Thought I ought to get to know all your friends. You know, beforehand. And your family. After all, soon they'll be my friends and family too."

"Mmm," murmured Sarah, sipping her drink.

"Your sisters are such darlings, aren't they?" said George, settling down beside her. They'd had them both over, Connie with her husband and Phyllida with her latest, a marine biologist she had picked up in Crete. Predictably, George had charmed them all. "You don't know how lucky you girls are," he said at one point, as Phyllida was recounting a childhood anecdote. Everyone looked at him askance. "To be part of a family, I mean," he explained. "Only child, me. And Susie, my first wife, well, she was orphaned when she was ten. We had no children, of course, sadly. And somehow, travelling as much as I did, I never really had time for friendships. Until now." He reached out to take Sarah's hand. "That's why I can't believe my luck, finding Sarah. Being welcomed into her family, meeting all her friends. Just can't get enough of it." Sarah squeezed his hand in return, moved. Her sisters looked on with envy.

Now George was ferreting around down the side of the sofa. "I've got a surprise for you, my darling," he said, lifting up a sheaf of papers. "I know we've just had the house done out for the wedding, but I thought, maybe, when we get back from Africa, we might consider this ..." He flourished a glossy brochure featuring a huge house in luxuriant, manicured gardens.

"Good heavens," said Sarah, "isn't that ...?"

"Yes, Bridgefold House," said George on a note of triumph. "Just come on the market. Popped in to see it this morning. It's got a fantastic view across the valley, beautiful studio for you, six bedrooms –"

"Six!"

" – and only a quarter of a mile away. Still near all your friends, and big enough to entertain whenever we want to. I thought, you know, new life, new house. Really be able to stamp our character on it."

"But I like it here," Sarah cried, unable to stop herself. "I love it. And we've just spent all that money."

"That'll only add to its value, darling," said George. "And, forgive me, but this is very much your house, with your memories and your history. I want somewhere we can both make our own. Does that sound so very unreasonable?"

Mandy phoned. "How's it going, you jammy so-and-so?"

"How's what going? My love life, the wedding, my work?"

"Whatever."

"Fantastic, sorted, non-existent, in that order."

"You're not working?" Mandy sounded surprised. Concerned.

"Oh, you know, bits and bobs. But no, not really. Too much going on. I feel a bit mean shutting the studio door and leaving George to his own devices."

"God, Sarah, that doesn't sound like you. Up with the lark and working feverishly until someone dragged you away to force some food down you. Remember?"

"Yes," said Sarah, "yes, I do."

The line hummed with silence.

"Perhaps," said Mandy gently at length, "you should lay down a few ground rules?"

George couldn't have been more understanding. Sarah couldn't have felt meaner.

"Darling, of course you must work. It's what you do. It's what you are. I'd never forgive myself if I thought that I was responsible for stopping your creativity. God, I don't want you thinking you can't paint when you want to. And I so love watching you work."

They agreed Sarah would paint on Tuesdays, Wednesdays and Fridays. Once the wedding was over. To seal their bargain, George bought her a bright red sports car.

The marquee billowed gently in the soft breeze, as dawn broke over the garden. The birds sang her a wedding day anthem. It felt strange to be standing alone at the bedroom window, the house to herself. Strange but restful. George, proper as ever, was staying the night with friends ("So quaint," said Katie. "Give him a big kiss from me. See you tomorrow. Love you, Ma."). Sarah's dress hung on the wardrobe door, beautiful, perfect. Wispy clouds hung in a china blue sky. A sudden hunger overtook her and, throwing on an old dressing gown, she hurried down the stairs and out into the garden, past the great white ship moored on the lawn and down to studio at the bottom of the garden. She pulled open the familiar oak door, anticipating the heady mixture of smells, paint, canvas, dust. Emptiness greeted her. Not a trace of her work or tools remained; the floor was swept clean around the massive packing cases, each stencilled in George's careful hand: Studio, Bridgefold House.

Sarah closed the door. The garden lay silent in the pure morning air, but for the dying notes of the dawn chorus. She walked slowly across the dewy grass, up the newly carpeted stairs, into her luxurious bedroom, pulled out a sweatshirt and jeans from the bottom of her wardrobe and slipped her bare feet into a pair of shabby deck shoes. Her wedding dress swayed slightly on its hanger as if affronted by the disturbance. The keys to her battered old car still hung on the rack in the kitchen. She grabbed them, slipped an apple into her bag, and then, crunching across the gravel, slid into the driver's seat and headed west.

COME OUT TO PLAY

"Don't stare," my mum says when we pass one of those funny kids in the street. "You mustn't judge by appearances." His dad's got him in a pushchair, but he looks way too big for it. He's got a nice smile though, if a bit dribbly. "OK," I say, smiling back at him and I slide my hand free of hers, because one of my mates might see us. Later, when I've kicked all the rubbish under my bed so it looks sort of tidy, she lets me go out.

We're down by the railway line and everyone's being very cocky, as cocky as you can be when there's no grown-ups and no-one wants to be the first to say we shouldn't be there at all. Little bits of gravel jab our feet inside our sandals, scuffed and dusty from the building site we've run through like Indians, dodging from one shadowy hidey-hole to another as if a posse of cowboys is on our tail. We keep an eye on the old man with the watery eyes who sits propped against the rickety shed by the road, cowering from the sun. From time to time, he rustles his paper and turns his head to spit, big gobs of yellow stuff that glisten in the grass beside him. The grass is all dry and brittle. He hasn't seen us.

Terry's got a stick of rock his Nan brought back from Hunstanton. It's pink outside and white inside and all of us want the chance to bite into it sideways and suck a piece into holes, the edges sharp inside our bulging cheeks so when we laugh sugar spit runs out of our mouths and we gulp it back. But Terry's holding on to the rock, twisting and untwisting the cellophane at either end, and watching us all through his hard little eyes, while ours flick from his face to the rock, back and forth, back and forth. No-one's going to crack and ask him.

Linda, cleaner than the rest of us as usual, in her Marks and Spencer blouse and pleated skirt, socks neat but dusted with dirt, sits on an abandoned tyre and stares unblinkingly at Terry as if she can force him into sharing the rock. She beckons me over and as she cups her hands around my ear, her fingers are damp upon my face, the plaster on her thumb snagging my hair.

"Promise him a kiss for a bit of rock," she whispers, then giggles, watching me with a 'dare you' face, kind of disgusted. I pull away, stuffing my hand into my mouth as I stifle my laughter, tasting the flakes of rust from the wire we forced our way through to get to our den. Terry tenses, like my dog when he thinks something's about to happen. Linda catches my eye and we laugh even harder.

Suddenly Carl is beside us, his face all fizzy with excitement, his stammer worse than ever. He's hissing and trying to catch his breath at the same time, his features all scrambled like a scribble with the effort of getting the words out. I see Terry watching him with a mean look on his face as if he'd like to stamp on his brother, rub him away and out of his life. I feel sorry for Carl, sorry for him being the way he is, sorry that he has Terry for a brother. But a little worm inside me wriggles with relief that he's not my brother, no matter what my mum says. He stutters and shudders, his thin shoulders heaving, but finally we get some sense out of him. All thoughts of Terry's stupid rock disappear as we creep along the narrow trail Carl has forced through the undergrowth and then tiptoe to below the window ledge of the wooden hut beside the line, which he has just discovered. We crouch down, silent but for our ragged, frightened breath.

Linda squats beside me, legs apart, and I can see her navy school knickers in the shadows at the top of her white thighs. Her hand snakes out from under her skirt and finds mine as we hold our breath together, listening hard. The shed is rocking, vibrating as if someone is banging something time and time again, not something hard, but soft like a pillow, and all the while we can hear a low, steady series of grunts. Linda is biting her lip, knowing like me that we shouldn't be there and that we shouldn't be listening. I look over to where the boys are crouched. Carl has his mouth half open, tongue poking out, lips glistening with spit. Beside him, Terry, still clutching the stick of rock, has his head to one side, and he is frowning as if there is something he is trying to remember. Then all of a sudden, he jerks his head back and a strange look creeps over his face, a horrible look that makes me shiver, but I don't know why. It's the sort of expression grown-ups have when they don't want to say something because we're around. I don't want to be there any more. I want to run home, I need a wee, I want Mum to grab my arm and tell me off and send me to my room. Silently, I get to my feet and pull Linda up beside me. We turn to creep away, but Terry lunges across his brother and grabs my ankle. It frightens me. I cry out.

The noise inside the hut stops. Terry's hand freezes on my ankle; I can feel it slippery on my hot skin. There is a bang like metal dropped on concrete, then a huge man emerges round the side of the hut, a huge, red-faced man in shorts and vest, running with sweat. He shouts out in surprise, or anger. He takes a step towards Terry who scrambles up and leaps backwards, losing his footing on the slippery gravel and floundering like someone trying to stand upright in a rough sea and then our gasps of terror are drowned out by the scream of the train rounding the bend, the rails rattling, and Terry falling, falling with his arms circling like sails, backwards down the bank where the line strikes sparks in the sun and the noise is enormous, filling our heads and our voices are silenced in our throats as time stops and there is nothing but the train and the sky and the thud thud thud of the wheels slamming into the metal and then the growing silence as the final carriage thunders by and disappears up the line, leaving behind only the faintly singing, faintly ringing rails.

And, impossibly, Terry is standing white and shaking the other side of the line. The man makes a move towards him and Terry's legs start to move and with a wobbly stagger, he picks up speed and begins running. The man hollers, "Oi!" but Terry's gone, up the far bank, through the fence and off into the scrubland that borders the park. I want to be sick and my pants feel damp between my legs. Linda is sobbing, her eyes pink and raw, her mouth red and wet as though it's full of blood. Carl is still sitting with his back to the hut, his hands raised in front of his face as though he is expecting, waiting, for the man to hit him. The man spins round and Linda and I both scream and I shout, "Run!" and we tear off, the twigs and thorns snatching at our clothes and raking our legs. We run and run, tears blinding us, the salty taste of snot choking us. I turn to look back, expecting to see Carl behind us, but he's not there. I stop. Ahead, Linda is a blur of blue and white. She doesn't look back. I think of Carl, his puny little body, his sad, twisted little face. My heart is pounding in my chest as if it will burst. I wipe the snot from my nose with the back of my hand, then wipe that on my shorts. My breath is all choppy as I start back towards the hut.

Carl's gone. I stand in the bushes to the side of the hut, gulping for air, my skin all prickly. The empty rails lie baking in the sun at the bottom of the embankment, like nothing's happened. Then comes the judder of Carl's voice, stopping and starting, then a high-pitched laugh. Carl's. It is coming from inside the hut. I don't want to be here. I want to go home. I creep forward and up to the window, and then, inch by inch, I raise my head to look in. Carl is strapped onto a low metal machine, sort of sitting down. The man is crouched in front of him and seems to be miming something. Carl is pulling feebly on a metal bar he is holding in both hands. I look beyond them to the far side of the hut and see another machine, like the one Mum bought last Christmas for Dad, which lies unused in the garage. I hear the man clapping and laughing and Carl crowing with delight. I walk round to the front of the hut and as my shadow falls onto the concrete the man turns round.

He doesn't look frightening now. He just looks very large, very hot and very sweaty. He has quite a nice smile. He looks a bit embarrassed, like he's been up to something. There are tools in the corner of the shed, spades, pickaxes, metal bars. A bright orange jacket with black sleeves hangs on a hook.

"Caught me out, you have," he says. "I didn't ought to have this stuff here, by rights. Still, what's the harm, eh? You been poking around, have you?"

I shake my head.

"Mind you, I ought to report you, by rights. Trespassing. As for that other lad ... bloody lucky, if you ask me ..." he trails off. I nod.

Carl gets off the rowing machine, and with one regretful look over his shoulder, comes to stand beside me. He takes my hand and we turn to go.

"Half a mo," says the man and he makes his way sideways like a crab down the bank and bends over to pick something up. He trudges back up the gravel to where we stand in the doorway.

"Here," he says, snapping the rock across his massive thigh and handing us half each. "Looks like your mate dropped something. Off you go, now, and don't let me find you here again. Mum's the word. OK?"

"OK," I say and tug Carl's arm.

"Oi, you. Girlie," the man shouts after us. "You be sure and look after that brother of yours." I go to say something, but the man's already walking back into the hut. Carl's funny little face looks up at me, eyes squinting in the sun, and he smiles. I don't smile back, but I keep hold of his hand and start to walk. Then, not even bothering to peel off the cellophane, we both stick the rock into our mouths and begin to suck.

Seventy Times Seven

"He could charm the birds off the trees," sniffed my Aunt Vera, eyeing my father over the top of her Picture Post. She was right. He was charming. Charming but, I realised as I got older, sly. The slyness only occurred to you later, when the headiness of his charm had dissipated and left a faint sense of disappointment in its wake, an uneasy feeling you had been duped. It was never strong enough for expression, just a little pinprick nagging away at the back of your mind. Somehow, he always knew when the elastic of your goodwill had stretched to the limit and in he would bound, that unforgettable smile on his lips and the deep, brown laughing eyes and you would be left feeling mean and spiteful. But so glad he was back.

Women, certain women, loved him. And he loved them. Oh, not like that. No, against all the odds, he was utterly monogamous. My mother never had a moment's worry on that score, even if she had to share him all through their marriage with the breathy, giggly women with whom he would so shamelessly flirt. But every now and then, if you knew what to look for, you would see a look exchanged between them, so swift you could miss it in the blink of an eye, as if she were saying, "Go on, then, it does no harm", while he would give a helpless shrug, "What can one do?" And sometimes, deep in the night, through the fog of sleep, I would hear them laughing in their warm cocoon of blankets and the hot-smelling sheets, under the rose-pink eiderdown, and wish I was there, snuggled between them, safe.

His charm worked on men too. Big bluff chaps in tweeds and Viyella shirts would watch benignly as their wives fluttered around him, hearty laughs at the ready for his knowing wink. Wallets opened as if by magic, with no embarrassment and no unpleasantness if loans were repaid a little late, or, sometimes, not at all. He danced lightly through the quicksands of debt, never leaving a footprint long enough to suck him down. Until the day he trod a little too heavily.

They came for him one bright, irresponsible March morning when the weather teased and mocked anyone intent on stepping outside. One minute sunny, the next glowering with heavy rain-clogged clouds scudding across a dark sky. As my mother opened the door on two grave rain-coated detectives (although she didn't know that then), the heavens gave one convulsive shudder and then haemorrhaged violently. The rain drummed ferociously on the tiled path where weeds shouldered the stones aside and gushed through our broken guttering in an unforgiving stream, straight on to the brim of the unlikely felt hat sported by one of them. In later years, I could never watch the old black and white police dramas with their broad-shouldered policemen, replete with homburgs, grim-faced on the doorstep without a momentary bowel-churning recollection of my father's nemesis. This despite the fact that I had been at school at the time and had only been able to piece together a manufactured memory from the mosaic of my mother's whispered remarks, dropped like confetti in the following days over tea and stale digestives with one or other of her scandal-seeking, gloating relatives. Like my sniffing aunt, they had never liked my father, although had been pleased enough to bathe in his reflected glory and share in his good fortune. I hated them with their mean hooded eyes and viper tongues. I hate them still.

They packed me off while he was awaiting trial. Banished to the cold, grey flock-wallpapered bungalow of a spinster aunt, eking out a dismal existence in a seaside town far away. Angry seas crashed on esplanades crumbling like cake where pinch-faced girls pushed their grizzling babies along in the wind, skirts flattened against their legs, hair whipped into their eyes and mouths. I went back years later and nothing had changed but the size of the girls, now bloated with fat and sugar, but with the same dead look in their eyes.

Uprooted from friends, I was adrift in a school peopled by the younger brothers and sisters of those girls, thin-faced, blank-eyed kids who mistrusted my foreign ways. Even the teachers seemed small-minded and parochial, contemptuous of London and metropolitan life and glad to while away their lives in that bleached and undemanding town. I was distant, haughty, seething with unfocused rage and self-pity. Letters arrived weekly from my mother – meagre, spiritless epistles, as dry as railway timetables. My father was never mentioned and, unless my taciturn aunt intercepted my mail, as far as I can remember, he never wrote. Her letters detailed meals eaten, clothes worn, the weather, with no trace of her former vitality and irrepressible good humour. Except it wasn't irrepressible, was it? It had been repressed, ironed out of her by my father's shame. My adolescence was blighted by the cancer of bitterness inside me, all my memories tainted by his betrayal. I came to dread my mother's monthly visits, the three of us sitting in awkward silence in the cheerless front room while my aunt nudged a plate of Battenburg and Rich

Teas towards my mother who would unfailingly refuse them with an upraised palm. My eyes fixed firmly on the floor, I answered my mother's stilted questions about my schoolwork and classmates monosyllabically, begrudging every word I forced through my lips. Our partings were brittle affairs, half-hearted attempts at an embrace, her dry lips brushing my frowning forehead. I think we both sighed with relief when the peeling green door was shut on her retreating figure as she made for the station.

When my father was released from prison three years later, I pleaded exams and the disruption of my education as the excuse for not returning home. I had grown used to my undemanding aunt, with her colourless home and bland meals. I had lost both my taste for the sparkle and fizz of my earlier years and also my knack for friendship. I wasn't unhappy or bullied, just ignored. Distance had eroded my bonds of friendship: in the days before texts and mobiles, how many young girls would persevere with letter writing? I put those recollections of carefree but intense friendships into the expanding trunk called 'My father's fault' and settled into self-indulgent loneliness.

The immediate homecoming delayed, I secured a holiday and Saturday job in a local newsagent who was not too particular about verifying my true age. Now I had a ready excuse not to go home at weekends and school holidays. With their precarious financial situation, my parents were in no position to argue. I needed the money. The one time they both came to visit me, I stood in the shadows watching them pace to and fro under the clock where we had agreed to meet, as they anxiously scanned the faces of the passers-by. I was pleased to see that they no longer touched one another with the unconscious ease I remembered, as if each had fed on the other to maintain their high spirits. My father looked smaller, frailer and had lost that questing, roguish look in his eye. His inner fire had been extinguished. He looked beaten. And I was glad, exultant even. Finally, despairingly, they took one last look up at the clock, then trudged back to the platform to catch the train home, my mother not even waiting for him to catch up with her. After that, she visited alone.

And then she died. Suddenly, no warning, at the kitchen sink. I wasn't there, of course. Like all the momentous events in my life, I was elsewhere. So it fell to my aunt, white with shock, to run to the front door as I walked up the path and stand there, mute with pity. I stopped, looked at her and just said, "Which one?" and when she said, "Your mother" I merely nodded and slid past her into the gloomy hall. I went to my room, dry-eyed, and sat on the bed. So, I thought, now he's a murderer, too.

It is two-thirty. Two-thirty on a cold Sunday afternoon in March. Scraps of rubbish and discarded newspapers skip and dance down the street in the biting wind. The light struggles through the thin curtains to smear the dusty surfaces in my bed sitting room. I am reading in fits and starts, reading a book the papers insist will uplift and inspire me. I could do with a bit of uplifting and inspiration. The hopes that brought me scuttling back to London as soon as I finished sixth form have dwindled over the last five years into faintly flickering flames, licking feebly around my feet. The ridiculous idea of university, in the face of no money and my aunt's unyielding opposition, has died; I'm trapped now in my latest job as a waitress in a coffee bar off Oxford Street. I wipe the tables with a

63

savagery my boss mistakes for diligence and sullenly repel the occasional attempts at flirting made by the faded men who sit alone, sipping their tasteless coffee. My meagre salary would hardly allow the renting of one small room in a multiply-occupied house in London, but my aunt, in her final gesture of wordless affection, had contacted an old school friend in whose basement I now live, paying an exorbitant, but non-market, rent for the privilege of being in Bloomsbury. The gracious streets, almost silent on a Sunday, allow the luxury of lonely, dream-filled walks, treading in the footsteps of the ghosts of others, like me, lonely, like me, bitter. Or so I like to think. But I'm twenty-three; I've much to learn.

The doorbell gives its feeble buzz, disturbing the somnolence of my afternoon. I almost don't answer it. My landlady is away. I've no friends, none to speak of. Through the thick mottled glass of the outer door, I can see a slim shadow, nothing more. The bell rings again. I uncoil myself from the sofa and pad over to the door in my socks. Despite the constant reminders in the papers, I remain careless of my safety; I don't engage the chain, I just open the door. An old man stands on the step, rail thin, unshaven, swaying slightly. A drunk, I think with irritation. I go to shut the door, but he puts out a skeletal hand to grasp the jamb, to stop himself falling.

"Yes?" I say, coldly. I note with a clinical detachment that I haven't stepped forward to support him, help him in any way. All I want him to do is go, stagger off into the silent street and disappear. But even as I think this, he gently subsides like a sigh on the threshold and crumples at my feet. There is nothing to do then but place a hand under his elbow and pull him carefully upright and inside out of the vicious wind. I lever him onto a wooden chair and, once confident he is not going to topple off, go to the sink to run him a glass of water. He sips it slowly, working the liquid round his mouth. Standing over him, I see the thin, greasy strands of grey hair plastered across a skull spattered with the brown stigmata of age. He finishes the glass and I take it from his hand.

"Thanks," he says in a croak, like someone who hasn't spoken for a while. As I go to turn away, his bony hand reaches out and stays my departure, its wrinkled skin apologetic against my fresh young flesh. "Thanks, Josie."

I don't flinch, I don't start, I'm not that sort. I knew anyway. Knew the way you know something without the need for words. I keep my voice steady.

"What do you want?" I say.

He's eaten very little: a few biscuits, half an apple which I cut up for him the way Mum used to do for me when I was ill. But there's some colour in his cheeks now and even some life back in his eyes. I watch him as he slowly chews the food, moving it round his mouth as if it's strange to him, foreign. He doesn't look at me, just concentrates on the worn, frayed rug at his feet. His shoes are scuffed, although they were decent enough once. Despite the shabby shirt, he still sports a tie, inevitably, I note with reluctant amusement, for a club he never belonged to. His trousers are shiny at the knees and, I guess, the seat; they hang from his thin legs like the clothes of a much larger man. Was he always this small? The years have been savage to him, tearing out his hair, scoring his cheeks with deep fissures of worry and privation. If he were not my father, I might feel pity.

I get up from the sofa without a word, take his plate and go to make us both a cup of tea. One and a half sugars. I give him the mug with the picture of the Coronation I found at the back of the cupboard when I moved in. The Queen's face is crazed and the cheap gold rim is almost worn away. He takes it gingerly and nods his thanks.

"Sorry. Sorry," he mumbles into the mug then looks up for the first time, really looks at me. I see something – shock? bewilderment? – flit across his features just for a second before his lizard lids drop, wiping the familiar face away to leave this prematurely aged stranger once more. I say nothing, sip my tea. And wait.

"Shouldn't have come. No, had to. Had to see you. No-one else since ... Frightened, I was frightened. Thought you'd throw me out." He looks me full in the face again. The ghost of my father confronts me. I know what he wants me to say. I won't. I won't say anything.

"I don't blame you for hating me."

Well, that's good, then.

"Hate myself. Killed her. Your mum. Killed her with shame. Knew you were ashamed of me, why wouldn't you be, just a kid. Sent you away. Stole your childhood."

Spare me the violins, I think.

"Come to say ... I don't know. What good's sorry? What good's anything now? Thought, wondered if you mightn't be curious. I was. Wanted to see how you'd grown up. Turned out. You're like your mother. Beautiful."

"Well, she's not beautiful now, is she?" I snap before I can stop myself. His eyes widen and then, incredibly, he smiles. Because he's got me to speak? I feel tricked. I look away.

"You want me gone. OK. Fair enough. Look at me, wrecked. Bloody wreck. Secondhand clothes. Can you imagine?"

This time, I do smile. Yes, I can imagine. I can imagine how mortifying it must be for a man like my father to wear some else's cast-offs, impregnated with another man's sweat and worse, the itch and scratch of used clothes against skin that had known cashmere and silk. He catches my eye and gives a rueful, self-deprecating grin. The old opportunism asserts itself, however weakly. He licks his lips in anticipation and sits a little straighter in his chair.

"OK. Be brief. That's the ticket. Strike while the iron etcetera. This is how it is. Just give it to you straight. Got about three months. So they say. They, the doctors. Makes me weak, but I can manage. Thing is, they want me in some home. Nowhere else to go. But I've got plans, Josie, plans I can't work on locked away with a load of corpses, plans for you. No, don't laugh. Listen, there's favours to call in, debts to be repaid. To me, Josie. For you. Just need somewhere ..." He sees my eyes widen. "Not here. I can see that now. But we could find a place –"

I explode with laughter, can't help myself.

"With you? You want me to live with you?"

He doesn't laugh with me. He simply holds my gaze and waits until I stop.

"Yes," he says, calm as you like. "That's the idea. Three months, that's all. Three months to make things up to you, give you something back."

"But I don't want you back. I don't want you in my life," I cry, wanting to see the hurt in his eyes. Except that it doesn't come. He shakes his head instead and struggles to his feet.

"No. Fair dos. Worth a try. Still, I got to see you after all this time, so that's a bonus. I'd like to have seen you happier. I thought, I don't know, perhaps there'll be some man, someone to make you happy. There isn't, is there? No, thought not. I know you don't believe me, but I swear I'd give anything to undo what I did to you and your mother. Best I can do in the circumstances is skedaddle." He shrugs himself back into his coat and makes for the door.

Skedaddle. That's what undoes me. Skedaddle. One of his chipper, nonsense words, one only he could get away with without sounding like an RAF buffoon in a B movie. I find myself on my feet, my hand on the door.

"Wait."

He grew younger with every word. The years dropped away like falling plaster. His skin lost its grey tinge and, as the colour returned to his cheeks, his eyes began to dance. I was enchanted, laughing in spite of myself, alive for the first time in years. Outside the window, a sparrow perched on the sill, looking on.

LOVE-LIES-BLEEDING

The body is cold when she finds it, the lips drawn back a little from the teeth, sightless eyes fixed upon infinity, a damp patch in the crotch. *That chair'll have to go*, her first thought. It doesn't frighten her, the body: startles her, yes, only in that she had thought the room empty. And it is empty: the intruder is both there and not there. She stands for a moment beside the hearth searching the vacant face, the beaky nose, sharpened with age, the faint mottling on the jawline, gone soft. A small scar beside the mouth, white against the unnatural, muddied tan. That almost brings a smile, then, with a stabbing shaft of memory, the old anger flares. She tries to will it away. It's too late for all that now.

She shivers, not with fear or revulsion, but because the room is chilly even on this bright October day. A solid, stolid woman, heavy ankles and a nagging back, she strokes the hairs upon her chin, lets out a long breath and shakes her head with something that might be regret, might be irritation. Floors to swab, the windows to do this week, and now this. She's not a woman for histrionics, not prone to panic. Not at her age. She'll do upstairs first.

"Why did you not ring sooner?" The doctor is brusque, his lunch interrupted. The woman shrugs. What's an hour here or there? It not as if there was anything to be done. But she's cleaned the rest of the place, wants to do this room now. "Name?" he asks, pen poised. She shakes her head, "Dunno." He starts, astonishment replacing the frown. "You don't know?" She doesn't reply, instead turning away to busy herself with the dusting, handling the fragile figurines with surprising delicacy.

The doctor is dumbfounded. He takes rapid stock. "This is not your house then?" Her eyes sweep round the room, its expensive swagged curtains, the antique furniture: she raises a scornful eyebrow.

"Right. So you're just the cleaner? And you've no idea who this is?" For answer, she turns again to her task. The doctor fishes in a pocket for his mobile.

The police take over. She answers their questions monosyllabically, an eye on the clock. Mrs Morgan will think she's not coming, and there'll be gripes. The body has been removed to the morgue; she wishes now she'd given it a longer look, given it more – she searches for the word – more *respect*. The carpet round the chair is soiled by muddy boots – and worse. There's to be a post-mortem: she's heard the policemen whispering in the hallway, glancing occasionally in her direction. ("Apparently she cleans all over the village.") She adjusts her bosom, affronted.

"Where are Mr and Mrs Jukes, did you say?" They've at least established who owns the house.

"I didn't say." She's watched enough dramas on the telly: she knows they try to catch you out.

The detective gives her a baleful look and says with studied patience, "Where are they, do you happen to know?"

She gives the question serious thought, examining it for traps, tonguing her dentures the while. "France, mebbe."

The detective scribbles a note. "Holiday? Would you have an address?"

"No."

He waits. The silence lengthens. "Then how do you ...?"

"They pays me upfront. A son drops by to keep an eye."
They circle each other like a pair of boxers.

"And do you have ..."

"No." She thinks the son lives in London, but won't
swear to it. All she knows is, he's a dribbler: the downstairs
loo floor always needs a going over when he's been in.
Once, he forgot to flush, the dirty devil. None of this is
shared with the detective.

Finally, "When did you last see them, Mrs
Clatterton?" (It's Clatterson, but she's not going to give him
the satisfaction.)

Another lengthy pause. "August. Or could have been
July." Suddenly, she volunteers, "They'll be back for
Christmas. They always come for Christmas." There's some
satisfaction in seeing the look of surprise on his face.
College or no college, he clearly doesn't know the ways of
the rich.

"All right if I shift that chair?" Without waiting for an
answer, she heaves herself to her feet and goes to move it.
He leaps up and bars her way.

"Evidence, Mrs Clatterton."

"Ah." That'll be the DNA, then. Never mind the smell of
wee which is getting stronger by the minute. Be a bugger to
get that out of the carpet.

Late afternoon, she is rolling out pastry in her cramped,
spotless kitchen, capable hands crimping the edges of the
pie. Sidney comes in, dour, sweaty after a day in the fields,
bringing with him the smell of earth and manure. "All
right?" It is not a question.

"All right."

She pours him a mug of tea, dense, bitter from long standing and stirs in two sugars. He takes it without a word and goes through to the hall to collect the paper. She hears him stop in the passage, imagines the headline, and then there is the snick of the sitting room door and the sudden shout of the telly. She brushes the pie with egg and lovingly places it in the oven.

They eat their supper in silence, the paper between them on the oil-cloth like a challenge. The meat is tender, the kidneys meltingly fragrant. Lambs' kidneys, that's the trick. Worth that bit extra. The ticking of the kitchen clock sounds unnaturally loud, as does the scrape and chink of their cutlery. He pushes his empty plate away, grunts something she reads as thanks but then instead of getting up to fetch his ciggies, nudges the paper an inch or so in her direction. "One of yours, innit?" She nods, willing him to leave it. "Weren't that the house where that boy never come back, after the war? Fetched up in Australia, I heard. Weird, though, some stranger turning up dead. What's that about then?"

She shrugs, stacks the plates and carries them over to the sink. Behind her, his suspicion weights the air. Let him just go and watch the news, leave her to her thoughts. Hot water scalds her hand: she almost welcomes the pain. She squirts washing-up liquid into the bowl, scrubs the plates over and over, waiting for him to make a move. Finally, he gives up. The sitting room door bangs shut and she is alone. A long, juddering sigh escapes her; she grips the edge of the sink in relief. A cat leaps onto the windowsill, startling her. On heat and no mistake: she's yowling and preparing to spray – not this close to the house, she's not.

A smart rap on the window and the cat shoots off into the bushes. The garden is darkening into shades of black and purple as the sun goes down; high on the hill, the single oak is silhouetted against the dusk.

An image explodes in her head, an image she has spent all day trying to suppress. She tries to focus on her reflection in the dark glass, face set, mouth tight, fighting the tears that press hotly against her lids. She can't stay here, needs air, needs space. Heeling her slippers off, she slides aching feet into broken work shoes and, snatching up an old anorak, slips out of the back door. It creaks as she pulls it to. Squirt of WD40, that's the answer. She'll sort it in the morning.

The lavender bush releases a smudge of late, drowsy bees as she brushes past. A bat or swift – she is not sure which, it moves so fast – arcs the sky above her. Stopping at the gate, she snaps off a handful of amaranthus blooms, all the garden offers this late in the year. It's too dark now to see the colours clearly. Appropriate at least, she thinks wryly, wondering if she's gone doolally. She's always loved her garden, knows her flowers, knows their connotations. Everlasting love indeed: some hope. Yet her fingers tighten round the stems. Then, arthritic knees protesting, she starts to climb the hill towards the tree.

Over fifty years since she last took the path, but it could have been yesterday. She doesn't need the moonlight; her feet find the way with ease. Wind ruffles her thinning grey hair, but her mind sees a cloud of unruly auburn curls against the blue of a cotton dress. Reaching the summit, heart pounding, sweat beading her forehead, she leans back against the trunk to catch her breath. Must be barmy, she thinks, struggling up here at this time of night.

At my age. Must be losing my marbles. She stoops and lays the flowers at the base of the tree.

Below her in the valley, one house stands out white and bright in the spill from a streetlamp. Once – long before these newcomers arrived with their fancy ways and their money – it looked like the family who lived there, shabby, unloved. The heavy oak door, now restored and lustrous with beeswax thanks to years of her elbow grease, opened then with the same key she keeps in her purse. The satisfying clunk as the tumblers turn every week and she steps over the threshold still gives her a secret pleasure. Not, as Sidney believes, because she swans round the empty house, playing Lady Muck. No, it's for the past, the echoes of those feverish whispers and the hot, desperate kisses exchanged in front of the hearth one stolen afternoon half a century before.

Above her head, the branches murmur and creak. The ground is cushioned now, as then, with leaves and twigs that always caught in her tangled hair. She'd sit impatiently on the ground as he teased them out before they descended, warily, separately, trying to look as if they'd just been out for a walk. "Never known such a girl for taking the air," her father used to say. She had blushed furiously, sick with guilt, giddy with love.

It couldn't last, not in a place like that; people always knew your business, no matter how careful you were. And he was wild, the boy – "a bad lot, the whole family", as her father never tired of saying. It didn't last. The war came, sweeping up all the young men and carrying them away. They didn't need much persuading to enlist: travel and adventure beckoned. Working the land or seeing the world? Not much of a contest. The chance of a new life, of starting afresh. That last evening, words exhausted, they sat in silence under the great tree, she, mute with misery, tracing their initials in the leaf mould with a stick. Suddenly, he pulled her backwards into his arms. Her hand flew up in surprise, the twig catching him beside the mouth. He cried out as a bubble of jewel-bright blood bloomed by his lip.

"Scarred me for life, you have," he said on a broken laugh. They clung to each other.

"Just so's you don't forget me," she said.

"Forget you? Fat chance. Anyway, I'll be back before you know it."

"Promise?"

For answer, he pressed his lips to hers, his salty blood flooding her mouth. The next day he was gone.

Tomorrow, they'll be back with their questions, she knows that. That smartarse detective, he'll be back for sure. Couple of days, maybe sooner – given all that clever technology they use nowadays – they'll identify him. They'll find his key. Sidney won't be the only one who'll remember him, remember them together, most likely. There'll be whispers and fingers pointed and God knows what.

But tonight, he's hers, her secret still. Tonight, all bitterness spent, she can mourn the life that might have been, a promise kept and a red-headed girl in a pale blue dress, with the taste of blood in her mouth.

Restless Pillows

"You've done it again!"

"What, pray?"

"Don't you 'what, pray' me, you insufferable little prig. Pinched my bloody storyline, that's what!"

Charlotte took hold of Emily's long braid and pulled savagely. Her sister, lying across the bed reading a dog-eared copy of *Punch*, screamed and lashed out with her legs, catching Anne, who was sitting quietly at her desk, a glancing blow on the shin. Emily snatched up one of her pencils and hurled it at Charlotte, now trembling and red with rage, in the doorway. The pencil missed Charlotte, ricocheted off the doorjamb and catapulted into the bedroom opposite, hitting the comatose Branwell on the cheek. For a moment, all three sisters held their breath, waiting for their brother to lurch out in his customary drug-fuelled confusion, smelling of stale alcohol and even staler clothes, threatening random violence. But mercifully all was silence. Charlotte tiptoed across the landing and pulled his door shut.

"You are an unprincipled cow," she hissed at Emily, who was massaging her skull and darting venomous looks at her.

The Rev Patrick Bronte's head appeared at the bend in the stairs. "Girls, girls, what on earth is going on? I'm trying to listen to the Afternoon Play, for heaven's sake."

"Sorry, Papa," chorused the girls as one.

"Anyway, Charlie," called her father, "I thought you wanted to hear it."

Charlotte wrinkled her nose and shouted back down the stairs at her father's retreating back. "Nah, it's one of Saint Jane's ghastly little vignettes of middle-class life, according to the Radio Times. Can't bear the woman."

"Okey dokey." He shuffled back to his study, contemplating the sheer bloody nuisance of three premenstrual women and a cokehead son under one roof.

Anne, ever the peacemaker, looked up from the laptop where she had just typed and then almost instantaneously deleted 'Alice was beginning to get very tired of sitting by her sister on the bank', and said, "Come on, stop sulking, no point rowing. Kiss and make up, won't you?"

Emily rolled over on the bed and stared up at the ceiling, mulishly. She scowled at the cracked plaster above her head and the damp patch in the corner which, now she looked at it more closely, resembled nothing so much as the ugly face of Charlie's boyfriend, Arthur Nicholls.

"I was only glancing at them," she said, appealing to Anne's soft nature. Charlotte was leaning against the wall, ferociously chewing on a hangnail. "I wasn't out to steal any ideas, honestly, just checking we weren't going to overlap, that's all."

"Yeah, right," said Charlotte sulkily, but her earlier rage was dispelled and she could feel her usual lassitude creeping over her. She looked out at the rain-sodden moors that stretched as far as the horizon and sighed, then said half-heartedly, "Just leave my files alone, OK? And if I find any of my characters in your next book, I'll throttle you."

"Whatever," said Emily and closed her eyes. A more companionable silence fell in the room, punctuated only by Anne's occasional typing. Sudden inspiration hit her and she bent to the keyboard. 'It was the best of times, it was *the worst of times'*, she typed, but as soon as she saw it on the page, it looked wrong, ponderously repetitive. She highlighted it and pressed Delete. Emily yawned, stretching her arms above her head. "What I want to know," she said to no-one in particular, "is how that Dickens bloke gets so much of his stuff published and we have to live in this godforsaken hole, probably snuffing it before anyone takes any notice of us."

Anne stopped pecking at the keyboard and sat back, considering. Of the three of them, she was always the one to think things through before she spoke. Charlotte was rooting through her underwear drawer looking for a clean handkerchief. Art was due round later and she supposed she'd have to go through all that tedious coquetry and eye-dabbing malarkey again.

"I suppose," said Anne at length, "that firstly, he's a man and no matter what Mary Wollstonecraft says, we're still hobbled by our sex."

"By sex, certainly," interrupted Charlotte grimly, thinking of Art's awkward fumbles under her corsets in the drawing room, once the others so considerately left them alone.

"And secondly," said Anne, ignoring Charlotte's comment, "he writes about really meaty subjects and huge themes and we mainly witter on about emotions and love and stuff like that."

"Witter!" roared Charlotte. "I don't bloody witter and nor does Em. Mr Rochester – well, admittedly, he seems a bit of a wimp at first – but he charges into that burning building and Heathcliff's all man, red in tooth and claw. No-one can accuse *our* heroines of being soppy. Not like that Pamela creature or ..." she trailed off, suddenly uncomfortable.

"Mine?" said Anne, quietly, and turned back to the computer. Her thin shoulders were eloquent in their distress and she was suddenly convulsed by a short, painful cough into her lace-edged handkerchief which was, predictably, bright with blood as she pulled it away and dabbed at her lips.

Charlotte was instant contrition. She rushed over to her youngest sister and flung her arms around her. Anne stiffened. Charlie was always one for the grand gesture, flouncing around the place and playing the drama queen, although Em could run her a close second at times.

"God, it's freezing," said Emily. "I wish someone would hurry up and invent central heating."

"And tampons," said Charlotte.

"And earphones," thought Anne, stoically trying to shut out the sound of her sisters' voices. She knew why Charlie was in a mood: she was waiting for her turn on the laptop. Em had already had her hour and Anne's had another ten minutes to run: she was damned if she was going to give in as usual and let Charlotte take over early. She banged away at the keyboard stolidly: '*As Gregor Samsa awoke one morning from uneasy dreams he found himself transformed in his bed into a gigantic insect*'. Dear God, she thought as she swiftly erased it in a kind of panic, I am definitely losing it. Where the hell did that come from? Nothing was coming easily today and the words seemed leaden and forced. She started again: '*Last night I dreamt*' and then immediately deleted the words. No, this heroine wasn't a dreamer, she was a feisty doer, independent, headstrong and vibrant. She wouldn't drift around like a wet Thursday in Heckmondswick. Anne's fingers hovered over the keyboard and then she found herself turning round and saying, "I've had an idea."

Emily lazily opened her eyes and looked over at her. Charlotte stopped picking at the ice on the windowpane and raised a questioning eyebrow. Anne felt herself prickle with heat at the unaccustomed attention.

"What if we wrote something together? Instead of each of us trying to find variations on the same theme."

"What? Rain, wind and blighted love?" said Charlotte bitterly.

"With Gothic overtones," said Emily.

"No, listen," said Anne, warming to her theme. "What if we wrote about a whole host of characters, say a lot of different people living in the same street, on a sort of rolling basis? There might be crises and sudden excitements, which dominate the action for a while, but then that reaches some sort of resolution and another issue comes to the fore."

The other two thought for a few moments.

"I suppose," said Charlotte slowly, "you could have a mix of comedy and tragedy, couldn't you?" As the others looked puzzled, she went on, "I mean exaggerate some characters a bit for comic effect and then weave in catastrophes like a railway bridge collapsing or some stables catching fire and one of the leading characters getting trapped by a roof falling in."

"Isn't that a bit derivative?" said Emily with some asperity. She secretly thought herself the most able of the three of them and Charlotte's success with *Jane Eyre* had irked her more than she cared to admit.

Anne was tapping her teeth with her pencil. "The trouble is," she said regretfully, "we're a bit limited, living round here. I mean, we don't really know many people, do we? And isn't it poor people who live in streets? I think it sounds a bit, well, common."

"Bugger that," said Emily. "If we'd paid the slightest heed to the advice in that distance learning course we did on creative writing, we'd never have written anything. Write what you know – what a load of bollocks. No, I reckon we've got something here. Let's choose somewhere no-one would want to go and write about that."

"What, like Manchester?" said Charlotte.

"Or the East End of London," said Emily. "That sounds fairly grim. Write about the sort of people no-one is ever likely to meet and we can be as ridiculous as we like and no-one will be able to say it's not realistic, because they won't have a clue. We could start with some description of the roofs of hovels with pigeons and cobbles and loads of poor people hurrying along in those things people wear in kitchens."

"Hairnets?" said Anne doubtfully.

"No, no, wait a minute – pinnies," crowed Charlotte. "No, but they could wear hairnets too. With those round cylinders in their hair." They all fell about at the thought of the benighted peasantry in floral and gingham pinafores cavorting in the streets, then, the idea taking root, their voices overlapped as they chimed in with ideas and names and plot lines. Anne typed furiously as they spoke.

"There could be a sort of central meeting place ... like a shop."

"Or a public house." This from Anne, with a moue of distaste.

"Called ... The Rover's Return or ..."

"The Queen Victoria!"

"Some disreputable characters with vulgar names. Les ... Den ..."

"Albert Matlock!"

"Tatlock's better. It's sharper. Sharples! Ena – that's a very common name – Ena Sharples ..."

"She could have a friend Minnie ... Minnie Cauldwell –"

Emily lowered her voice and beckoned her sisters closer.

"What if ..." her cheeks were flushed, "what if we had some of those, you know ..."

"What? What?" chorused Charlotte and Anne, bewildered.

Emily blushed, a less than attractive sight on her sallow face. "You know, those ... lady boys. And those girls who ..."

"What? What?" Her sisters' brief sojourns in boarding schools, and Charlotte's weekly tussles with Arthur Nicholls appeared to have borne little fruit in the way of sexual enlightenment. Emily bent closer to their adjacent ears and whispered.

"Oh my God!" Anne fell back in horror. "What, they ...?" Emily nodded triumphantly, feeling herself very much a woman of the world.

"This," she said to her sisters, "could go on forever. If old Dickens can spin out his yarns for months in the mags, there's no reason why we couldn't do the same. All we need to do is convince our publishers."

Anne pulled a face. "The trouble is, we'd be switching genres, wouldn't we? You know what they're like. They already think we're men as it is."

Charlotte frowned. "It's a bummer, isn't it?" she said. "You know, bloody Dickens has really cornered the weekly instalment market. Libraries are awash with drippy

Austen-type drivel with their oh-so-genteel heroines fannying about in Bath and London. We need a new way of getting to our readers."

Emily suddenly sat bolt upright.

"What if," she said, her eyes alight with excitement, "what if they weren't *readers* at all. What if ... someone invented some way of making people *see* what we're talking about. Not on paper but like a sort of play. But instead of it happening just once in one place, it was, I don't know, sort of *beamed* into people's homes. Everywhere."

Charlotte and Anne looked at Emily's face, now mottled with patches of hectic colour. They both recognised and dreaded the fever which had surely taken hold of her.

"Oh, Em," said Charlotte surprisingly gently, "get real."

NIGHTHAWKS

She is drawn to the light. It promises a haven in the inky night and she has been happy here. Her heels click across the linoleum and no-one looks up. A woman, coatless, hatless, gloveless, without a purse at 3 a.m., and no-one looks up. It's her kind of place.

She slides onto her favourite stool, tight against the far wall. Without a word, Ricky slams down the lever on the coffee machine. The bitter aroma punches air that is wreathed with cigarette smoke. Ignoring her upraised hand, he places an empty cup in front of her and grunts, "On the house", then pours in a steady stream of black salvation. She flicks her eyes around the diner, faltering for an instant as she snags her gaze on the man sitting across the counter. He is looking at Ricky, at the machine, at the counter, at anything but her.

The coffee scorches her lips. She doesn't care, almost relishes the burn. It rakes the sides of her throat as she swallows but the tears that rise are not on account of the pain. Not that pain anyway. The fingers of her left hand unfurl to reveal the ring that has been clenched so tightly since she fled the apartment. The imprint of the claws around the tiny diamonds is etched deep into her palm, highlighted with pinpricks of blood. The same blood that smears the inside of her wrist and the bathroom floor. As she holds the ring up to the harsh, bright, night-time light, its brilliance breaks through the muddy smears, refracted by her tears. She tips her head back and forces them to retreat.

A man materialises on the stool alongside her. Another of the anonymous, shiftless people who walk these dark streets. The place is almost empty, but he chooses this stool, this close. She knows what he's after. He lights a cigarette, takes a long pull, then pushes the packet along the counter toward her.

"Smoke?"

Shaking her head, she drops her left hand down beside her, out of sight.

He persists. "You from round here?"

She turns her slow gaze upon him, takes in the mottled flesh of his face, the tic in his right eye, the lust she can almost taste, along with his whiskey-laden breath. Evenly, she says, "You're wasting your time, buddy."

Anger flares briefly in his eyes, then Ricky breaks the moment, refilling her cup.

"You OK?" he says, wiping down the counter, the long sweep of his muscular arms a not-so-veiled warning to the stranger. She nods, with a brief flash of a smile that illuminates her face, gaunt in the overhead lighting. Ricky settles himself comfortably on his strong legs in front of the man and says tonelessly, "You want something, mister?"

The air sings with tension, as the man weighs up the odds. Then he shrugs, releasing with the movement a heady mix of booze, smoke and sweat, a sweat of both staleness and fear. Ricky does not move.

"I said, you want something?"

"Yeah," says the stranger, a little telltale break in his voice. "Gimme a beer." Ricky keeps his eyes locked on the man's face as he locates a glass under the counter by touch and, reaching behind him, takes a beer from the cooler. He flips the cap off the beer; the liquid foams and hisses in the neck and bubbles down the side of the glistening bottle. He places it with great deliberation in front of the man who pours it into the glass with an unsteady hand.

Greta watches the encounter between the two men, with a kind of distanced interest as if the harsh white lights were intensifying its meaning and importance. Men, always men. Wanting, demanding, taking. Hot, greedy hands on her body. Hands that can hurt as easily as caress. Hands that curl into fists. She finds her own hands clenched at the thought. A small involuntary laugh slips out. The man across the counter looks up for an instant, frowning. Beside her, the bum knocks back his beer and stands up, slapping a note down, then walking out without a word.

"Scum," says Ricky, picking up the money. "He bother you?" Then his eyes fall on Greta's hands, which she is now flexing and straightening in front of her. "You been in a fight?" She glances down. The stain on her wrist looks dirty but unmistakable under the lights.

"Something like that."

Ricky swears softly under his breath. They go back a long way, him and Greta, but this is more than their usual exchange of intimacies, in the safe cocoon of the diner. He leans toward her across the counter, resting on his elbows, and lowering his voice says, "Trouble, honey?"

It undoes her. The kindness, the concern. The tears tremble in her eyes and then begin to fall. He reaches out and gently thumbs them away. She doesn't flinch as he touches her face, the only man she would let do that.

"Hey," she says, and tries a smile, but the muscles seem frozen. She's forgotten how to make them work.

"Wanna tell me?" he says. She notices how the blackness outside is reflected in the dark pools of his eyes, eyes that have seen so much and yet contain no judgment. And he is still looking at her, a little puzzled, but with a slowly dawning comprehension. He lets out a low, incredulous whistle.

"Oh, baby," he says, waiting, hoping she will dispel the thought that has formed like a stone in his heart, with one of her familiar easy laughs. But it does not come. As she locks eyes with him, he sees that she has gone somewhere beyond any words of comfort. He reaches out and takes her hand in his and waits. She wets her lips. Her voice, when it comes, is thin, frail like an old woman's, and as she speaks, he can see the barriers she has built around herself crack and craze.

"You can only take so much, see. There's only so much room for ..." she hesitates as she searches for the right, the exact, word, "... accommodation. And I reached the bottom, Ricky, reached the absolute goddam pit tonight, where there's nothing but fear and nowhere to go. You know?"

He nods, not trusting himself to speak.

"Could have borne it, carried on, let him do what he does, what he makes me do. But – not Ruby. Not my baby. She's ten years old, for Chrissakes! I come back from – you know – and he's got her in one of my dresses and he's painting her lips, he's painting her little baby lips. And Ruby's laughing and posing and he looks up and I can see, there's no pity there, there's just a calculation: how much? And Ruby's standing there beside him with such a look of defiance on her face and she ... she throws her arms around his neck and gives him a fat kiss, all the while her eyes glued to mine. And then he says to her, 'You go next door, baby, 'cos Mom and me need a little chat.' And you know what? She does. She don't argue, she just gives him a little smile that is, oh, so knowing, so private, and then I know. I know what he's done, what he's doing to her and know I have to get him out, make him go or ..."

She is willing him to understand, her face ashen in the unforgiving light. He exhales a little shakily and gestures her with a nod of his head to continue. The nails of her right hand bite into his flesh.

"I'm opening my purse, I'm pulling out every dollar, every cent and I'm promising him, promising everything, even this, my mother's ring, the only thing of value I got. He's angry at first. So angry I think he's going to lash out. Face so ugly, all bunched with rage. And then he laughs. He grabs my hand and he jams the ring back on my finger and he says ... he says ..." The tears are now leaking down her cheeks, raining on to the thin fabric of her dress. "He says, 'Sweetie, that little diamond in there will fetch me much more than your tacky little chips. I'm going to mine her for all she's worth'. And I know he means every filthy word he says. He just laughs in my face and turns away." She swallows and her eyes stare unwaveringly into his. "So I hit him. I had my hand around the lamp somehow and as he went toward her room, I hit him, real hard, on the back of the head. And he fell like a stone. Didn't cry out, he just ... crumpled. I was so scared Ruby would come out of her room and see him. So I dragged him into the bathroom and ..." Her face convulses at the memory. "He's still breathing. He starts moaning and I know what will happen if he ... I just want my baby to be safe, you know? And there's the razor by the tub and I pick it up and, Ricky, I just did it ... I just did it."

A long low shudder escapes her and she puts a shaking hand to her mouth. Her eyes glisten with tears, but they no longer fall. A hardness enters her voice.

"Weren't no accident. The lamp, yeah. But not ... the other. I knew what I was doing. But I couldn't stop myself. Not if I wanted to save Ruby." Her eyes are like flint in the whiteness of her face.

"It's OK, it's OK," says Ricky, knowing that it is not, that it will never be OK again. "Where's Ruby now?"

"With a neighbour, girl in the next apartment. I ran into her bedroom and just dragged her out. I told her Mommy had to go see someone in a hurry and she couldn't stay there by herself because Eddie had ... wasn't there anymore. She still had the lipstick on, Ricky, all around her mouth. She looked dirty, you know? My little baby looked like a tramp. I just had to get away, just clear my head. And I didn't know where else to go."

"You did right," says Ricky. "You did right."

Greta steps off the stool. She straightens her dress, wipes a hand over her face and moves in an instant out of their private world into reality. Across the bar, the solitary man slips a note under his beer glass and quietly makes for the door. As he opens it, cold air eddies around their ankles. The man pauses just outside the diner and his unreadable face is briefly illuminated as his lighter flares in the darkness.

Greta's hand reaches out to pick up the ring, then she stops and pushes it across the counter to Ricky. "Will you look after this for me? Give it to Ruby for me?"

He goes to say something, then thinks better of it. "Yeah. Sure," he says, pocketing it. "You going to be all right?"

89

She shrugs and a smile dances for a moment across her face. For that second, the old, tough Greta is back. "Me? You bet," she says and begins to walk toward the exit, head high. In the doorway, she pauses. "Hey, Ricky? You're a pal." Then she is gone, almost swallowed up by the blackness. Like a ghost, her image flickers on the far side of the window. Then the stranger is beside her and all Ricky can see is the blur of Greta's face turned up toward his, his hand on her arm and her brief nod as he holds up his badge. He thinks he can hear the muffled snap of the cuffs as the couple melts into the night.

Making Trouble In An Empty House

I did my best to break the news tactfully – I mean, there's no point upsetting people unnecessarily, is there? Although, I must admit, I think anyone would have been upset, being picked out like that.

"Did they actually mention me by name?" she whispered nervously. "I mean, actually say my name?" That's one thing I've noticed about Betty over the years: the way she peppers her speech with 'actually'. Actually this, actually that. It's very irritating, but you can't say anything, can you? She was doing that awful thing with her jaw, working it the way Gordon Brown does when he's under pressure. His is due to a rugby injury, so I've read; I think hers is just nerves. I would love to have reassured her but really, what can you do? I knew what I'd heard.

"Not by name," I said. "Not as such. But I heard him say, the mousy little one with untidy hair. Couldn't think who else he meant. No offence."

Her hand flew up to her head. She looked stricken. "Is it? Untidy?"

I pulled a noncommittal face, but thought, do you not look in the mirror, woman? Let's face it, in the current economic climate, you can't afford to stand out. You don't want to be noticed – well, not for the wrong reasons. You want to keep your head down (your neat, well-groomed head), get on with your work and keep busy. Particularly when there's new management and they've got everyone in their sights.

"Was it just me?" She grabbed my arm; she was getting a bit hysterical, to be frank. I thought I caught Mr Deans raising his head a tad above his screen: she's a penetrating voice, Betty, when she gets agitated. He wouldn't like that. I gave him a brief wave, just in case, but he was looking away. "Well," I said, "I thought I also heard mention of Eric and Clive." This time her hand flew to her breast: aye, aye, I thought, so she *does* have a soft spot for Clive. I'd long suspected it, the way they so often seemed to end up at the same table at lunchtime.

"Oh, but ... oh but, I can't afford to –"

"What, stand around gossiping? No, neither can I. Let's get on, shall we?" I said, walking smartly back to my desk and busying myself with the monthly returns. I knew she'd be over as soon as the coast was clear, but frankly I really didn't have anything more to tell her. That wretched Dawn had come in right in the middle of the conversation, so I'd had to flush. I don't think anyone realises what you can hear through the wall from that end cubicle when the Ladies is empty and the cistern's stopped refilling. I waited a bit, but Dawn was obviously there for the duration, fiddling with her hair, no doubt, as per. I said to her once, "You'll ruin your hair with all that muck you put on it." She gave me one of her looks and said, all hoity-toity, "They're *products*, as a matter of fact," as if that made any difference. I still think she looks tarty, sitting there in her tight tops in Reception. I mean, who wants to see that when they're waiting for an appointment?

The news – well, rumour really, I suppose – was all round the office by the end of the day. That's the drawback of emails, in my opinion. Too many people with too much time on their hands. Of course, this is precisely what the new brooms'll be on the lookout for. I caught Felicity playing Patience, if you please, on her computer the other day. "Nice work if you can get it," I said, just as Mr Deans was passing. She had the good grace to blush and said very loudly – almost rudely, I thought – "It's my lunch hour, thank you, Moira." I gave a little laugh, just to show there were no hard feelings and then pointed out she'd missed the eight of clubs. I've always been good at cards.

Anyway, come five o'clock, I was fully expecting Betty to rush down the stairs after me, but there she was, glued to her screen, as I walked past to get my coat. Clive was also still in the middle of something – certainly too busy to look up as I brushed by his desk. It's all very well Betty holding a torch for him, but he's a married man and should know better than lead on a spinster like her. "Night, all," I said cheerfully, glancing back at my tidy desk, all the papers in neat piles ready for the following week. I raised a hand to Mr Deans but he was on the phone. I'm not sure about him yet, it's early days, but I get the feeling he's cottoning on pretty quickly to how our little section operates. I said to him Day One, "If you need to know anything, don't hesitate to ask." He looked so grateful. I've never had much time for Clive but he had the decency to say, "That's right, Moira knows everything there is to know about this place." Corporate memory, it's called: I've been on a course. Corporate memory is important: prevents new people repeating old mistakes and ensures that the history of a company is preserved. Too many firms used to just chuck it all away, but it's my belief folk are getting much more canny these days. And I can't help thinking that that sort of knowledge will be invaluable in a recession.

I said as much to Eustace over supper. "Mark my words, once Mr Deans has had the chance to get his bearings, he'll be needing me to fill in the gaps for him. There's no-one who's been at Eastwoods longer than me."

"Self-evidently," said Eustace, poking around his back molar with his pinkie to dislodge a bit of bacon. He's always been a man of few words.

"Betty Ridgeways better watch her step," I said. "Sounds like she's for the chop, by all accounts. Mind, I've always thought she was a bit of a lead-swinger, forever having time off to look after that mother of hers. Not that I'm saying disabled people don't need caring for, but that leaves the rest of us to pick up her work, which I don't think is fair. I said as much to Mr Phelps before he left and he agreed with me."

Eustace nodded. "Is there pudding?" he asked. "Only I need to get on." That's Eustace all over, always working. Bit like me, I suppose; neither of us likes to let the grass grow. I sometimes joke that he spends more time in his shed than in does in the house, but it suits us both, being on the go. He'll often take a flask down the garden so he doesn't have to interrupt his work to come back in for a cup of tea. I mean, I would take him one, of course I would, but he likes his privacy does Eustace and I respect that. He pottered off directly after supper and I settled down to Eastenders with a box of Milk Tray left over from Christmas. I thought after the week I'd had, I deserved to put my feet up. I wondered if Betty and Clive were still beavering away at the office in the vain hope of impressing Mr Deans. As if he doesn't know the score. What he wants are employees who get on with the job and finish their work within the allotted hours. He said as much the day he arrived, when we were all a bit shell-shocked after Mr Phelps' abrupt departure. Work-life balance, he said, that's what we're after. Work hard, play hard and get the job done.

Monday morning, bang on the dot, I'm switching on my machine. Betty is already feverishly typing away, as if her life depends on it. "Been here all weekend, have you?" I call over gaily. I like to have a bit of laugh. She looks up and I almost gasp. She's been done. Her hair, that is. All the straggly bits are gone and it's looking really rather neat. Then I notice her blouse, which is definitely new. I smile inwardly. Left it a bit late, Betty, I think. Unless this is all for Clive's benefit. She doesn't say anything, just smiles weakly and returns to her work. I get myself a coffee while the machine warms up. Mr Deans comes out of his office and calls out in his nice American accent, "Please ensure you all read my email before 9.30." I scan it: "tough economic challenges ... difficult decisions ... reconfigurations ... streamlining ..." Oh dear, oh dear, poor old Betty.

"Moira?" Mr Deans is beside me. "Could I have a word?" I suppress a smile – it's never clever to look smug – and follow him into his office.

Dancing the Midnight Polka

My father was a gentle man. Yes. Gentle, that is the word, gentle, but with strength. A gentle strength from a gentleman. He never struck his children, never raised his voice. He left that to my mother. The past did not interest him. Only the future. The maybes, the possibles. He painted a world for us full of hope and opportunity and, like all children lapped in security and love, we grew careless of our blessings. We took unquestioningly and he gave us everything unquestioningly. We were so happy. So lucky.

We all left home eventually, moved away, created our own selfish worlds. We rang when it suited us, cadged meals when money was tight, ran home when our little lives imploded. Then, with his retirement, we noticed a change. His foreignness, his non-English qualities, which for our sakes, I think he played down in our childhood, began to come to the fore. He was uncharacteristically gloomy sometimes. He buried himself away in his study, surrounded by a mountain of books. Perhaps he simply had too much time on his hands, to think, to remember.

I rang one evening, steeped in self-pity, bruised in the aftermath of another failed relationship. He answered after a couple of rings. I pictured him at his desk, reading as usual, hunched over the page, a forbidden cigarette burning in the ashtray.

"Papa," I began, but he cut me off short. No greeting, no endearment.

"What do you know about Hungary?"

I was knocked off balance. "Hungary?"

"Yes, Hungary, the country." He sounded cross, impatient.

"I ... well, Budapest?"

"*Igen.* Yes, of course. What about it?"

I scrabbled in my memory for the vestiges of European history, geography.

"It's two cities really. Buda and Pest."

He repeated it, pronouncing it in his still heavy Hungarian accent.

"Good, yes. *Pest.*"

"And is it the Danube runs through it? Oh, and it's very popular for stag and hen dos."

"What?"

"Stag and hen parties, before a wedding. You know, cheap flights and that."

He snorted with disgust.

"What else?"

"I don't know ... part of the Soviet bloc?"

"And?"

"Oh God, goulash, Liszt – he's Hungarian, isn't he?"

"And Bartok, Kodaly, Erkel, Laszlo. Surely you've heard of Sir Georg Solti and Fritz Reiner?"

"I think so. Conductors, aren't they? What's all this –"

"Nothing. Nothing."

"Well, you never talked about it."

"You never asked."

I considered this for a moment. "But we're English."

"You're English, yes. English through and through."

"What else would I be? I don't know anything else."

"You don't know anything."

I cut the conversation short. Now was clearly not the time for confidences. He sounded distant, distracted. Old.

The following day, I called round. The flat looked dusty, unkempt. A woman came in twice a week, but I suspected Papa did not keep a close eye on her. She was a nice enough woman, a Bulgarian, I think. Ivanka, yes, that was it, Ivanka. Doubtless, he'd found her in the Hungarian café he frequented in Hampstead; that was where he seemed to meet most people. Certainly it was where he met both his wives after my mother, Katerina first, a permanently smiling Bulgarian, blessed like Ivanka with sturdy calves and strong forearms, then pale wispy Sofia who drifted wraithlike around the flat and then finally out of his life altogether. My mother Tzveta, still shrill and opinionated at seventy-five, lived her busy, noisy life in Hendon, surrounded by other widows and divorcees of her generation, buoyed up with outrage, imagined slights and copious amounts of tea.

Strange then, that given the frequency of his visits to The Sanctuary (*A Szentély* underneath in brackets in a tiny flourish) during our childhood and adolescence, he never took any of us there. "You would be bored, my darling," he would say, shrugging on his long overcoat. "A lot of old people, not for you." Did he come back different? Sad? I don't know, I was too caught up in my own dramas to notice.

Today, however, he looks troubled. He kisses me with his usual warmth and apologises for his behaviour the night before. "Something, nothing," he says when I press him. Little bits of his native tongue have crept back into his conversation. "*Szeretõ*," he murmurs into my hair, holding me close to his bony chest. "What?" I say, startled. He mutters something and goes into the kitchen to put the kettle on. I notice how stooped he is these days, weighed down with something he does not want to discuss. Or something I'm not sure I want him to discuss.

Watching him pottering round the old-fashioned kitchen, I try to make conversation, break the awkwardness.

"That woman is back at the tube station, Papa. You know, the one with the baby. Begging. I told you last week. They should do something."

"They?"

I hand him two mugs from the cupboard. "Yes, the authorities. Should do something about the baby at least. It's out in all weathers."

"The authorities," repeats my father heavily. "What should they do, exactly?"

I don't hear the tension, the anger in his voice. Blithely, I say, "I don't know. Take the baby. Look after it. She obviously can't."

My father slams the mugs on the counter. "Can't? No, I don't suppose she can. Have you spoken to her? This woman? No? I thought not. Well, I have. She has no home, no family. She moves from house to house, a few days here, a few days there. All she has is the baby."

I hold up my hands. "OK, OK, I'm sorry. I didn't know."

His eyes are burning. "Imagine. Just for one moment. Imagine what this is like. You think people lightly tear their roots from their own soil? No! You think they wake up one morning and think, yes, it would be so good to go begging on the streets of London with my little child?"

"No, Papa …"

"No. A strange country. Hostile. People who look away. People who look too hard. Contempt. Hatred. Occasionally, some pity. But pity is not what you want. Dignity, that is what you want. Dignity and warmth and family and a home and enough to eat. Is that so much to ask?" His hands are trembling. I take the spoon from him, gently, and begin spooning tea into the pot. The air is tense. I hear him rubbing his dry palms together, collecting himself.

"Papa –"

He sighs. "I am sorry. Things – things I thought I had left behind – they come back. Always. You can never escape, not really."

I stop what I am doing and go over to him, take his long, elegant hands in mine. I bend to kiss them. "What's happened?"

He hesitates a moment, his thoughts far away, then makes his mind up.

"I've had a letter," he says.

We are sitting in his study, both nursing mugs of tea. Beside him on the desk, teeters a huge pile of books, littered with post-it notes and bookmarks. Some are in English, but many are not and the scrawl on the notes is indecipherable. I have already emptied the overflowing ashtray into the kitchen bin. He goes to reach for his cigarettes, catches my look, withdraws his hand, smiling ruefully. "The young," he says. "So disapproving."

"Young?" I say. "I'm thirty-three, Papa. Charles is thirty-seven. And Andrew, for God's sake, Andrew is nearly forty."

He nods.

"A lifetime. No, two lifetimes."

"What do you mean?"

"Listen," he says, "I have a story for you. My story. You want to hear it?"

As he starts to speak, the years fall away from him, his skin tautens, eyes brighten and the young Tamás Szabó lives again.

"What I am telling you is about another world. A world apart from the shameful little you know of England," he holds up his hand to stop me as I go to protest, "your country of birth, my adopted country. Here people were emerging full of hope into the sunshine of a new world after the privations of the war. Yes, there was rationing, yes, housing was in short supply, but here, people could speak out, could argue, change things. Look what they did to Churchill – threw him out of office like a piece of useless old rubbish. New, fresh, exciting, that's what they wanted here as they rebuilt their country."

"I thought you were telling me about Hungary, Papa."

"Hungary, yes, but what you must understand is that we, I, knew nothing of this other world. It was kept from us. In Hungary, we also had come through the war but the Russians for us at least at first were our saviours. They saved us from the Nazis. So we thought. But then when it was over, the war, they stayed, and their puppets stayed. So. First we are liberated. Then we are dominated. It is not just Hungary. No, of course not. It is the story of many, many countries. Many peoples. You must understand this. Things creep up on you. You can get used to anything in time. It stops being appalling, terrifying – all the epithets we use to describe something that is very wrong – it becomes ... the way it is.

101

"And it is 1955. I am in my early twenties. Things are not easy but I have managed – against the odds – to carve out a career in chemistry. I am doing research at the university –"

"In Budapest?"

"*Igen*. Things have happened, of course, but –"

"Things, Papa?"

"Terrible things, to my family. To our friends. To everyone. But, no, they are not terrible to other Hungarians. They are commonplace. Daily. Atrocities, you would call them now."

"Like ...?"

"Things you might read about some African country today. People seized in the middle of the night. Beatings. Torture. Rapings."

"Rape? You mean ... people you knew?"

"Of course."

"Family?"

"My aunt. Yes. My cousin, a little boy, hiding in a cupboard while they, the Russians ... well. And my uncle taken away. Forever."

"My God, Papa ..."

"Yes, it is hard to credit, with your young people popping over there now for a weekend on a cheap flight, drinking, laughing, free as birds. But then, we were ground under the Soviet heel. Remember, Stalin, that monster, he only died in '53. Until then, the Russians held Hungary by the throat, like a vice. Merciless. His henchmen rule the country, take their orders from Moscow. But when he dies, well then, the world draws breath. We all feel it, the hope, the possibility of change. It's in the air. Of course no-one voices it. Not as such, we know the dangers, but there is a look, an eyebrow raised here, a half-smile there. It is as if after long winter, the ice is beginning to thaw and spring is waiting to burst through. Waiting. Impatient.

"Perhaps it is only with hindsight I see this. Perhaps in the moment, I am still crushed by the daily reality. The fear, always the fear of saying the wrong thing to the wrong person. Oh, they were very good, the Communists, at keeping us at each other's throats. Trust no-one. Tell no-one. That was how to keep safe. Even your friends ... how could you tell if they were trying to protect their own? Sometimes, you have to choose ..."

"Choose?"

"Sometimes, you have to step into the unknown. But sometimes, wonderful things can happen too." He pauses, head lifted as if trying to catch the sound of something in the wind. He smiles. "A rainy night. A sudden storm. The gutters are overflowing, like a river down the city streets. Running into the shelter of a shop doorway, eye on the clock because of the curfew. Ten minutes to reach home and it takes eight at a fast walk. And then she falls into the doorway too, laughing, shaking her wet hair and she turns and ... she looks at me. And I know. I know, as God is my witness, that this is the one. For now and always. The one."

I can scarcely breathe. He sits back and sinks into his chair, the vitality gone. He looks tired.

"Papa?" I whisper. "This is Mami? This is how you met Mami?"

He looks at me with the eyes of a stranger, puzzled. "Mami? No. God, no. You know I met her here, in England. No. This is Malika. My Malika." And I think I see tears glistening in his eyes before he turns away, reaching over to the desk and taking hold of a pile of typewritten sheets, stuffing them into an envelope. He is weary, now, exhausted. "Here. Take them. Read. My diary. I typed it up. It's all right," he says with a faint, sad smile. "You can read it. It's in English."

June 5 1956. I've never kept a diary before. But then I've never felt like this before. I suppose I shall have to find somewhere safe to hide it. Not just from Mother, but from the usual. What a country! But it's not the country I'm excited about. I know I should be. H. is always nagging at me at work. Tamás, he says, you can't bury your head in the sand, you've got to take action. I'm doing my work, I say, isn't that action? He looks at me pityingly, shovelling papers into his briefcase. I know he's lost people, we all have, but what can we do? H. says, Something, we can all do something and if enough of us do something, things will change. But my life has already changed.

Malika. Ma-li-ka. I can't stop saying it. It's like a little chant in my head as I walk to work, run up the steps, jump on the tram. We met in a doorway, just last week. It was raining, we were both soaked through. I can imagine Mother's reaction. In a doorway, Tamás? Is that quite respectable? Not respectable, no, but wonderful.

The way she smiles and her eyes sparkle. Her mouth, the shape of her mouth. She smells of gardenias. I know, because I asked her. I can't believe I'm writing these things.

June 12 1956. I'll never make a diarist. Too ill-disciplined. Look, it's a week since my last entry! Too much going on. We meet every evening after work, sit for hours (or so it seems) in the café at the end of the bridge. We talk and talk. It's like there isn't enough time to say all we want to say. Well, there isn't. I think I'm in love. No, I know it. I'm in love.

June 20 1956. H. tries to drag me off to a meeting this evening. You have to come, Tamás, he says. It's your duty. I tell him I have other responsibilities. I haven't told him about Malika, I haven't told anyone, she doesn't want me to. Why, I say, I want to tell everyone. But no, she says, it's our secret. She's made me promise.

This meeting, it's one of these Petofi gatherings. Writers and journalists, all taking a stand against the government. H. says Khrushchev made some speech about Stalin and the old days. Denounced him. In secret. More secrets. The world's full of them. H. says it's a coded message – the bear wants to lighten up, free things up. I'm not so sure. Why would they do that? They've got us exactly where they want us, Nagy out, that bully Rakosi in. Where's the lightening up in that? God, I hope no-one ever finds this.

June 28 1956. God, God, God. Now I know why Malika didn't want me to tell anyone about us. Why didn't she tell me sooner? She looked bruised – her eyes looked bruised – as she was telling me, holding my hand tight. She's married. Married. She has a husband. God. The poor bastard's in some camp in Siberia. Or she thinks he is. She has had two little scraps of paper from him in three years. Thrown over the wall in the hope someone will pick them up, send them on, despite the danger. The last one was eighteen months ago. Since then, nothing. She said, Tamás, Tamás darling, you mustn't think ... Well, I was thinking. But she's not like that, my Malika. She loves me.

She said they married young, too young. She says she's never felt like she does with me. She was crying. Took her back to her place. Missed the curfew. I stayed the night.

June 29 1956. H. was in a dreadful state this morning. He says there's a rumour about something terrible happening in Poland, a place called Poznan. Workers killed and wounded at some anti-Communist rally. Thousands of them. It's all rumour and counter-rumour at the moment. But faces are grave. All except mine. I had to hide my feelings from H. – he knows me too well. So this is Moscow lightening up, is it? I said. H. shook his head: Can't you feel it, Tamás? The ground shaking? Yes, I said. But I was thinking of Malika.

July 3 1956. Malika and I had a proper heart to heart this evening. Afterwards. She said, it's wrong, isn't it, to be this happy, with everything that's going on? Because H. had been right. About Poland. The iron fist had smashed down on them. Fifty of the workers at least killed. And still the rumbles continue here. It's like a pot with the fire lit. No matter how hard you ram the lid on, the pressure builds until it spills over. Then God help us. I want to be a part of it, *must* be a part of it, I see that, but at the same time, all I want to do is be with her. Malika. My love. I said to her, if you could, would you divorce him? I shouldn't have said that. A terrible thing to ask, with the poor man where he is. She didn't answer and I felt so ashamed.

August 4 1956. A month – it's been a month since my last entry. So much has happened. Oh, not with *us*. We are as we were, no, we're better, deeper, than that. I want to tell people, my mother, H. I want to say, there's this girl ... But she won't let me. She's right, I think. You tell someone something, you give them power over you. I know that.

Politically, things are getting hotter. I think it's something to do with the weather. Really. Hardly scientific but I think hot weather breeds hot heads. There have been fights, scuffles on the streets. The police are jumpy, coming down hard on anyone they think is up to no good. That shit Varga was hanging around the department one day, trying to engage H. in conversation. I pretended to be busy. I could hear him, dropping names and mentioning meetings he'd been to. He wants to know if H. is a Party member. That's a laugh. If he only knew. And me, I suppose he'll be wondering about me. Easy enough to check up, I'd have thought. H. said two more people disappeared last week. I didn't know what he meant. He got quite angry with me, quite violent. I don't mean physically, but he was furious. You can't avoid things forever, Tamás, he said, you can't live your life in a dream. No matter how irresistible she is. I felt sick. I said, who? Who do you mean? He said, don't take me for a fool, Tamás. You're a good man, but you're a crap liar. Then he got on with his work.

We've been working really hard on this big project. It's exciting work – groundbreaking. Every day, I am excited, more and more excited about what is emerging from our work. Anyway, the boss of bosses is convinced we're on the verge of something sensational. I'm sure of it. Someone said he's been invited to speak at an international conference about our work – so it must be important, perhaps more than we fully appreciate. Whether they let him go is another matter.

Malika and I have talking about the future. It's a sort of game we play. If you were free ... Only I mean free as an individual, she means free as a woman. That's not the same thing at all.

23 August 1956. I went to a meeting last night with H. All a bit cloak and dagger getting there. H. lead me down innumerable alleys and side-roads and I kept thinking we'd passed the same place several times. He was really nervous. Then we ducked into a little doorway and descended to a tiny cellar, full of men and cigarette smoke. I say men, there were a few women, but it was mainly men, student types. A lot of shouting. I felt quite old. They were brandishing a manifesto of sorts, with lots of demands, chief of which was to see Imre Nagy back in power. Unlikely, I'd have thought, in view of Poland, but there was much talk of 'the winds of change'. Fine words, but against the Soviet army? And our own? Let alone the AVO. I can't see them giving up their stranglehold. It was exhilarating, though, down there, felt as if change really might be possible. At the end, we sang *Stand Up, Hungarians*. I'd forgotten how powerful it is. When we got to the final line: *We swear never again the chains to bear,* there were tears in a lot of eyes. Then we stumbled out into the cold night air, one at a time, to disappear into the darkness of the sleeping city.

28 August 1956. Malika was frightened this evening. Someone had come to her office, asked if she had heard from her husband. He wouldn't give a name. She said no, she had no idea where he was, if he was dead or alive. "That's handy for your nice young man," he said as he left.

Neither of us spoke for a while after she told me. We just sat there, thinking. I was wondering if I should ask H. for advice.

14 September 1956. Mother asked me today where I go in the evenings. I said I had a lot of work on, getting the project finished. She said to me, you will be careful, won't you, Tamás? It was the way she said it that nearly undid me. I almost told her about Malika.

17 September 1956. H. is really on edge. He says one of his neighbours was beaten up by the AVO at the weekend. He's no idea why. The guy was in a bad way but wouldn't go to hospital. When H. went to check on him the following morning, he'd gone. His wife was crying and the kids. Let's hope he's somewhere safe. Varga's been back. He's getting bolder. I don't like him. Malika's late.

19 September 1956. Panic over.

24 September 1956. Fever pitch at work. Boss of bosses is definitely going to the conference. He's presenting a paper. The conference is in London, so H. and I were convinced that he'd never get permission. But apparently it's so prestigious, the authorities want him to go 'for the glory of Hungary'. It *is* exciting, because it means that some of our work will be seen, get recognition even, outside. In the free world. It seems funny writing that but that's exactly what it feels like – us in a cage, looking out at the rest of the world. And within the Hungarian cage, Malika and I are in a little cage of our own.

30 September 1956. Bit of a scare this evening. Got home to find my mother waiting for me in the hallway, this diary in her hand. My blood ran cold, really. I felt ice cold. She handed it to me. She said, you should be more careful, son, the back of the cistern is the first place they look. I couldn't speak. There'd been a leak and the old boy next door had come to look at it for her. He'd found it. Gave it to her without a word. What a way to live. He's solid, the old man, fought in the war. He won't tell anyone. I had to ask her. Have you read it? She looked at me as if I'd slapped her. Of course not, she snapped and hobbled back into the kitchen. I felt awful. But so relieved. I think the safest thing is to keep it with me. Or destroy it.

12 October 1956. I'm getting worse and worse at keeping this diary. Something about having it in my bag, I don't know. Not having much time on my own. And it's crazy, everything's crazy. We're working flat out to finish this piece of analysis – it's needed for this famous presentation. Everything is geared towards that. I said to H. the other day I feel I could recite it in my sleep. Outside, things are really getting hot. The whole city feels as if it's about to explode. People disappearing with greater frequency, beatings on the street in broad daylight. Half the population looks cowed – the older folk mainly – but the young ones, the students, it's almost as if they are asking for trouble. Everyone knows not to look at the police and the others, the ones you can tell are secret service, but the students! It's like they want to provoke them. H. has become very secretive, says the less I know the better. Know about what? We're both starting to feel exposed here in the department as non Party members. Varga's poison seems to have been very successful, most people have succumbed. Can't blame them, most of them have wives, families. But I have Malika.

14 October 1956. Snatching a quiet moment while I am waiting for Malika. Yesterday, afterwards, we were whispering to each other about our dreams. She said, where would you like to be if you could be anywhere in the world. With you, I said. No, she said, I mean would you want to live here in Hungary always? I said, no. It surprised me, and her. Because I didn't hesitate, just said, no, like that. And I realised it was true. I said, if I could go, with you – and Mother – leave this wretched country, I would. I'm tired of being afraid all the time. Not terrified, although that too occasionally, just afraid, like a dull ache in the belly, all the time. Afraid to speak too loud, afraid to voice opinions, afraid to trust people. Except me, she said. Of course, I said, except you. I'd trust you with my life. And I you, she said. And then a wave of hopelessness overwhelmed me. This secrecy, I'm sick of it. I want to walk out with her, her hand in mine, proud of her. Proud of us. How much longer can we go on like this?

The typing stopped halfway down the page. Just stopped. With the entry for 14 October 1956. Sitting on the sofa in my little flat, the images whirling round my head, I felt cheated. I looked in the envelope in case anything had been left behind when I pulled the papers out; it was empty. Glancing at my watch, I reached for the phone. It was nearly eleven, but Papa kept late hours. I knew he wouldn't be asleep. He answered on the second ring. Almost as if he had been waiting for my call.

"What happened? Why did you stop?"

"Let us say events overtook us."

"What events?"

"No, not on the phone. Come round tomorrow."

"No! I can't wait until tomorrow. I'll come now."

He didn't argue.

"OK. But take a taxi."

Speeding through the almost deserted London streets, the envelope on my lap, I stared out of the window, unseeing. Instead of the few people making their way home, of the pockets of light and conviviality in the pubs we passed, my head was full of the menacing silence of the dark Budapest streets, occasional figures huddled in doorways, the sudden noise that set the heart racing. I saw Tamás and Malika slip like shadows down alleyways, pausing in the shelter of the dark for a stolen kiss. I felt the heavy mantle of dread and suspicion that cloaked the waiting city, its cellars and abandoned buildings teeming with angry life, a secret world beneath the feet of the oppression. Papa was waiting for at the door, ushering me in without a word. Two mugs of tea stood steaming on the table in the study; he handed me one as I sat down, my mouth suddenly dry, my heart jumping. Papa settled himself in his buttoned leather chair.

"That was the last entry. That's why it stopped. I never wrote in it again."

"The last entry? Why? Why did you stop?"

"I left Hungary. The day after that entry. 15 October. I never went back."

"Never went back?"

My father closes his eyes for a moment, gathering his strength. I think what a fine looking man he still is, noble even.

"It is so hard to explain, Eve. So hard for someone like you who has known only freedom to understand what it was like for us. Listen.

"Malika and I, we spend the night together again. My mother perhaps is thinking I am working through the night. In the morning, I go to the university as usual, but the corridors are teeming with strangers. They look like AVO. People are grim-faced, white with shock. There is shouting, people running. H. is already there. He raises an eyebrow at me: ask nothing, it says. I get to my desk. Then suddenly, the Principal is there, in our office. We both leap to our feet. He is flustered, no, frightened. We know something is very wrong – we have never seen him before in our lowly department. He thrusts an envelope at us. Here, he says, Szabo and Hajdu, you are going to London, to the conference. Collect your papers now. Here are your passports and visas. There is a car outside, it will take you to the airport. The flight is in two hours. Do not let me down. H. and I are stunned. H. says, what about the Professor – but the Principal cuts us short. He jerks his head towards the doorway where a couple of men – AVO without a doubt – are standing and whispers, barely his moving his lips: The Professor has been taken away. There is a sharp intake of breath from H. Later, I realise he was not altogether surprised. I say: But, sir, we have no clothes … our families … The Principal steps back and for the benefit of onlookers he says loudly: There is money. You must go immediately. Your families will be informed. It is a

113

great honour for Hungary, this conference. You should be honoured also."

"My God. So, you just went ...?"

"We had to. It was incredible. Three hours later we were in the air, feverishly checking through the papers. I don't know why – we knew it by heart. H. and I had written most of it, done most of the work. And then H. put his hand on my arm and said softly, 'Tamás, are you going back?'"

"He meant to Hungary?"

"Yes." Papa puts his head back and looks up at the ceiling. His knuckles whiten as he grips the arms of the chair. I imagine him belted into the aircraft seat, his homeland far below him, flying towards freedom.

"But what about Malika?"

He sighs heavily. "I was young. In spite of everything, I was full of hope. I thought, she will find a way to join me. No-one knows we are lovers. She will find a way. You know, when you are young, you think everything is possible."

"And in London?"

"Oh, London! They put us up at a grand hotel. We have never seen such things – fine soap, huge soft towels – it is like a story, we cannot stop laughing, touching things. We walk out in the evenings, through the streets, and no-one stops us. H. says, don't be surprised if we are followed, but I don't care, it is so *csodálatos* – like a miracle – to be out in the open walking wherever we choose. We do the lecture, excusing the Professor's absence, as we have been instructed, as a sudden illness – it is a great success. And then I say to H. 'And now?' He knows what I mean. He shakes his head. 'No, I must go back. But you, you would be a fool to pass up this opportunity.' And I say, because I want to believe it, would you take a message back for me?

He says, to your mother? Two messages, I say. He laughs, ah! La belle dame? He is a kind man, my friend, a good man."

"So you stayed and he returned. And he gave Malika your message?"

My father stares at me for a long moment, then shakes his head. "*Nem.* No. He did not." His voice cracks. "When he landed, without me, he was arrested. I did not know of course for a long time. But he never got home. Never saw his family again. He was killed."

"Killed? Papa!"

"What we did not know, could not know, was that everything was about to explode. The authorities were anxious for the outside world to believe that everything was under control. That's why they wanted a Hungarian presence at this conference. But, things were not under control. The country was at boiling point. The harder they cracked down, the bolder people got. On October 23, students from the University began to march, calling for political freedom. Thousands marched, joined by workers, by housewives, everybody. The streets, they say, were bursting with people, singing, chanting, happy. There was no violence, not then."

"What about the police?"

"At first they watched. I believe they did not know what to do when it started. Then one group tore down the statue of Stalin and planted the Hungarian flag in what remained of the ogre's feet. You remember the Iraqis toppling Saddam's statue?"

I nod.

"Well, that is what it was like. That important. Earth-shattering. So it seemed. I only heard later, much later, from people who got out. But I see it, in my head. I hear the cries of joy. I picture the faces of my countrymen, lit with hope."

My father's face, too, is lit with an inner triumph, quickly replaced by sadness.

"But alas! It was short-lived. Within hours, the secret police – the AVO – opened fire on the protesters. A terrible riot, blood on the streets of Budapest. The gutters ran red. Indiscriminate, they didn't care. And the following day Khrushchev sent in the Russian tanks. But still the people rose up. For a few days, across the country, the symbols of oppression were destroyed. Imre Nagy took power, abolished the AVO – can you imagine? – and on 30 October the Russians withdrew. Was it foolish for the people to rejoice, to think they had won? They even turned to the UN for help."

"And did they? Help?"

"No. Their eyes were turned elsewhere. Egypt."

"Egypt?"

"Suez. The Suez Canal. You know what happened?"

"Sort of. But Hungary?"

"Left to its own devices. Oh, the bear does not like to be thwarted, to be challenged. You have heard of the domino effect? Well, first Poland, then Hungary. Khrushchev and his henchmen, they could not let Hungary break away. On 4 November, the Russians returned in full and bloody force. They crushed the Revolution. It took them about a week. The people, the students, Freedom Fighters, they had no proper weapons, but they fought and fought. So they say. Thousands died. Thousands more were put on trial, hundreds executed. The Moscow fist once more smashed the people into submission. Show trials. Torture. Nagy was executed for treason. One of many."

My father falls silent. Out in the hallway, the clock chimes midnight. I wet my lips.

"And Malika?"

His eyes darken.

"I don't know. I did not know. I believed H. would have given her my message somehow. I did manage to get news to my mother. But although many, many people managed to escape, it was very dangerous. And no word of Malika. The years went by. I settled here, married your mother. Assimilated. Or tried to. Put it from my mind. But Malika was always in my heart. And then, this extraordinary machine."

He pats his computer.

"The internet," I say.

"Yes. The wonderful worldwide web. All those tiny strands criss-crossing, interweaving, pulling the threads of the past into shape."

"You found her. Found out what happened to her? How?"

"I got talking to someone, an émigré, at the café a few months back. His brother had escaped to America at the end of the fifties. He told me of these wonderful Associations there, that support the Hungarian community. Write to them, he said, they may have something on their records. Email, he suggested. But I could not. Too brutal. Too impersonal. So I wrote. I wrote to them with Malika's name, where she used to live, the name of her husband. I felt sick. Sick and stupid. I had been too afraid to look for her before. I thought, it is more than fifty years. She will be dead. Better she is dead – for who could forgive me for what I did?"

He swallows hard, and tears tremble in his eyes. I take his hand.

"What happened, Papa?"

He tries a smile. "A letter. I got a letter from America. They have a system, they ask people if they are happy to have their contact details passed to others."

"She's alive?"

He nods, as a single tear tracks down his cheek.

"I think so. I think it is Malika. There is a telephone number. In Ohio."

"Have you ...?"

"No. I have not had the courage. What I know of this woman, this Malika in this letter, is that she remained in Hungary. Her husband was imprisoned in Siberia, was eventually released and they lived together until he died. Then in the sixties, the late sixties, she went to America and married again. Her second husband died last year."

"And you think this is definitely your Malika, Papa?"

"I want to think so. I want to think she had some happiness. I want to think I could ask her forgiveness."

"And you still love her, Papa?"

"I have always loved her."

The clock strikes the quarter hour.

"Do it, Papa. Ring her."

"No, I ..." Panic flares in his eyes. "It is too late. Tomorrow, perhaps."

"It's not too late in Ohio, Papa. It will be early evening. Do it. Dial the number."

"Fifty years, Eve," pleads my father, but I see his hand move towards the telephone. I wait.

He turns to the desk, lifts the receiver and begins with agonising slowness to dial the numbers, his finger running along the writing in front of him. I picture a neat kitchen, soft lighting, gingham curtains at the window. An old woman staring out into the night, erect, her face wrinkled with the years, but eyes still bright, still searching. As the telephone begins to ring, she sighs and makes for the living room.

My father's fist is clenched around the receiver. Neither of us can breathe. Far away on another continent, in another life, a phone rings and rings.

"Hello?" The voice is warm, clear down the line. It sounds foreign, East European. My father's body jerks as if an electric current has run through it. He snatches a breath, turns to me, his eyes dark and desperate. I put out a hand to urge him on, gently squeezing his arm.

His voice, when it comes, is barely more than a whisper.

"*Malika?*" he said, "*Az van Tamás.*"

There is silence, then a broken cry and a rush of words I cannot understand. Papa looks up at me, his face a shifting tapestry of joy and loss and redemption.

"What did she say?"

"She said," and now he is crying and laughing, "What took you so long?"

Fiat Lux

"Any ... minute ... it ... could be ... dismantled and ..."
The boy wriggled on his seat as if infested with worms.
"Dismantled and ... moved? Sir." Jenkins sat back,
exhausted, along with the rest of the class and their
teacher. Twenty-five pairs of eyes crept to the clock which
showed another thirty gruelling minutes would have to
crawl by before they could all escape. Donald stifled a sigh,
gathered his reserves, and wondered if any of this was
worth the effort.

"Hmmm ... *any minute*," he mused. "Does that sound
quite right, Jenkins?"

The boy, who, believing his ordeal over, had returned to
picking at a particularly satisfying scab on his elbow,
jerked upright. Four hundred volts could not have effected
a more dramatic response. "Sir?"

"*Any minute*? Have another look."

Jenkins stared blindly at the page, paralysed with
panic. Cribbing from Patel was all well and good, but only if
the little sod got things right, otherwise it was 50p down
the drain. The words dissolved into a senseless blur on the
page. Jenkins swallowed hard, thoughts ricocheting round
his brain like a trapped pigeon, while the class held its
collective breath. Old Vickers could go off like a rocket
sometimes and paid absolutely no heed to this PC corporal
punishment prohibition. If he felt like tweaking a boy, he'd
just go ahead and tweak. Most ears in the class bore
witness to this. The silence expanded like a bubble of
unexploded gum.

"Sir?" piped Porter's treble. Alone among his classmates, his voice refused resolutely to break to his unending misery and regret. This fact and his unapologetic nerdishness made him the butt of every jibe and practical joke going, anti-bullying policies notwithstanding. A groan ran round the room, while Jenkins breathed a silent prayer. "Would *'in a moment'* be better?"

"Indeed," said Donald, wondering why Porter's enthusiasm for the subject and his undoubted intelligence engendered only irritation, *'In a moment'* would be infinitely preferable. *'In a moment'* better captures the ongoing nature of this activity. Armies had to be able to move fast and speed was of the essence. Don't you agree, Jenkins?"

Jenkins, who had no idea what the old man was on about and was only grateful a tweaking seemed unlikely, nodded vigorously. "Sir. Oh yes, Sir. Absolutely."

"There, Porter," said Donald. "Even Jenkins finds your translation more apt. Even Jenkins who would not recognise a Roman onager if its entire arsenal were to be aimed in his direction. Thank you."

Porter's small frame suddenly jerked skyward as the boy behind gave him a hefty kick up his smart arse. Donald fleetingly considered intervening but then, to his surprise, discovered he simply couldn't be bothered. Double Latin with the third form not only on the last day of term but the last day of his entire teaching career too, seemed a punishment cruel and unusual for both him and the boys. He let it pass and looked out over the sea of apprehensive faces to select his next victim. The class, while apprehensive, seemed almost disappointed that the master's customary response was not forthcoming. Nothing like someone being subjected to a quick tweak to take the pressure off the rest of them. A ripple of unease shivered through the air, sending little spikes of vague alarm through brains both sentient and dormant.

Then Llewellyn, six foot one of suppurating acne and athlete's foot, rose from his desk, stirring the fug of sweat and oiliness that accompanied him everywhere like an invisible cloak. "Sir?" He was the sort of thick-knuckled boy who always sounded as if he had a cold. Adenoidal, most likely. The rest of the class and Donald stared in amazement. Surely Llewellyn, thicker than any plank, whose only purpose in life was to provide an immovable barrier on the rugby field, surely he wasn't about to contribute to the discussion of Roman field weaponry? He was not. No, he was doing something infinitely more dangerous. He was about to ask Mr Vickers a personal question. "Sir? Is it true that this is your last day? Like, ever?"

Several boys exchanged anxious if not astonished glances: this was really taking a chance. The old boy's temper was famously mercurial, one minute he would appear benevolence itself, the next he would erupt into a volcanic rage, usually because one of their number had transgressed some arcane rule in a Latin translation. They observed with trepidation the narrowing of the master's eyes, the pinching of the nostrils, while Llewellyn's bravado deflated rapidly. The adolescent hulk subsided on to his chair, which creaked under the weight. The hormonal cloud, at once bitter and sickly, slowly settled and the air cleared. Again, silence fell and lengthened. Had any boy been in possession of a pin – unlikely scenario – and dropped same, you would undoubtedly have heard it fall.

Donald Vickers suppressed his annoyance at the boy's temerity, wondering how he knew. He had asked the Head for no fuss, eschewed a leaving do and intended to slip quietly away after the Leavers' Assembly as unobtrusively as possible. He suspected that despite his best endeavours the Head would be unable to resist the temptation to exercise his fruity, unctuous best: "And now I have, with much gratitude and regret, to announce ..." But that possibility aside, he had been determined that forty years of unbroken service should end with no ceremony to mark their conclusion. Only now did he wonder why he had been so insistent upon the point.

He cleared his throat. The boys tensed. "As you have divined, Llewellyn, this is indeed, *like,* my final day of teaching." One or two titters greeted his ironic reply. Taking courage from this, another boy raised his hand to pose a supplementary. Coningsby was one of the brighter students who, although he would never have been foolish enough to admit this to his peers, quite liked Latin and had a certain respect for his master's stern defence of the language. "Sir? What will you do next, sir? When you" – he thought he'd risk it – "like, retire?"

Again, a surge of sniggers, quickly damped. They watched for the tell-tale signs: the pursed lips, the elevation of those untamed eyebrows. Had Coningsby gone too far? It seemed not, for the old man was now looking out across the playing fields where other, luckier, boys were enjoying an impromptu game of cricket. Except that, just at this moment, cricket was the last thing on Donald Vickers' mind.

Coningsby, unwittingly, had struck a painful nerve. This was the problem: Vickers really had no idea what he was going to do. He had his pension, he owned his modest flat overlooking the High Street, he had his books and ... well, that was about it. No wife (no, not gay, just unlucky), no family (or none that he wished to claim) and precious few friends. A couple of chaps he might chat with on his rare excursions to the pub, one or two acquaintances from the local History Society who infrequently invited him to dinner (when he took great pains to supply a really decent bottle of wine) and an old university friend with whom he had enjoyed several walking holidays in the Lake District over the years. Coningsby's innocent question had awoken the nagging thoughts he had been trying so hard to ignore: what exactly would the next – how many? Ten? Twenty? – years hold?

Turning back to the class, surprising himself, and breaking his own decades-long pedagogic rule, Donald spoke his mind. "I really haven't the faintest idea." And he smiled. It was an honest, open smile, a smile between equals. And then, to forestall the pitying looks he was sure would follow, he heard himself saying, "What would you suggest?"

The class was, to a boy, wholly taken aback by this turn of events. Old Vickers had never revealed *anything* about himself before. Not that they had been that interested, to be truthful; there were other more flamboyant masters – and even a couple of mistresses – to gossip and speculate about. When they thought about Mr Vickers – if they thought of him at all – they imagined him unmarried, judging by his old-fashioned, shapeless clothes and air of mild neglect. What he liked, what he loved – indeed, *who* he loved – were mysteries that few had ever bothered to dwell upon. But now faced with this undoubtedly sincere question, several of them realised that he had been a pretty decent teacher, with a passion for his subject few others matched, and that, in years to come, they would remember him, his thin, stooped frame, his sharp wit and odd words of Latin, long-buried, would float into their consciousness.

"Travel, sir, you could travel. Wherever you wanted." This from Rose, wiry, Jewish, with a love of geography. "Whenever you wanted. Especially off-peak," chipped in Greville, destined from birth to be a banker, who was already mentally surfing price comparison sites on the internet. "You could write a book, sir!" said Connors, top in English, who kept a vivid diary and wrote intense emotional poetry in secret. Donald raised a quizzical eyebrow. "About the Romans, sir. About their lives." "And their weapons, sir," shouted Jenkins, to much hilarity. "Especially the onagers!" A barrage of hoots. "What about visiting all three parts of Gaul?" suggested Vernier, defending his French roots which survived only in his surname. Dutifully, his classmates roared. "Or Italy!" cried Porter shrilly. "The Coliseum, sir! All those beautiful –" "Signoras!" yelled Llewellyn, revelling in the mayhem his impertinence had provoked. His interjection brought the house down; even Donald permitted himself a smile. Goodness, he thought suddenly, he was going to miss these boys, their enthusiasm for life, their irreverence. Glad as he had been to reach retirement, he now realised what they all meant to him, the studious, the truculent, the attentive, the infuriating, they and all their predecessors down the years. "Sir, sir!" yelled Greville through a storm of shouts and catcalls, "Travel in term time and you'd save shedloads!" "Shedloads? Would I indeed?" queried Donald wryly. As the banter continued and the excitement mounted, he found himself infected with their enthusiasm. He allowed his mind to wander: out of the classroom, across the town, the country, the Channel, the Continent. What was, after all, to stop him?

A hunger grew in Donald Vicker's lonely, shrivelled heart, for adventure, for discovery – who knew? – even for love. The boys were right: he could do whatever he wanted. He could go wherever he wanted. Nothing shackled him any longer – not duty, not responsibility, not safe, familiar routine. The first tentative shoots of a new beginning flowered, breaking through the shell he had so assiduously built around himself over four decades, eclipsing the years of duty, of timetables, of set books that until today had been his life. He thought – with a shiver of sudden pleasure – how quickly, how easily, it could all be dismantled.